I've travelled the world twice over,
Met the famous: saints and sinners,
Poets and artists, kings and queens,
Old stars and hopeful beginners,
I've been where no-one's been before,
Learned secrets from writers and cooks
All with one library ticket
To the wonderful world of books.

© Janice James.

The wisdom of the ages
Is there for you and me,
The wisdom of the ages,
In your local library.

There's large print books
And talking books,
For those who cannot see,
The wisdom of the ages,
It's fantastic, and it's free.

Written by Sam Wood, aged 92

AND NONE SHALL SLEEP

Jonathan Selkirk, a ruthless high-powered solicitor, is in little doubt that the letter suggesting he 'make a will' is intended to frighten him. Indeed, only hours later he is recovering in the Leek Cottage Hospital with a suspected heart attack. Detective Inspector Joanna Piercy is also at the hospital, and inadvertently finds herself at the scene of the crime. For late that night, Selkirk mysteriously disappears from his private room. The discovery of a dead body two days later leaves Joanna coping with a murder investigation.

PRISCILLA MASTERS

◆

AND NONE SHALL SLEEP

Complete and Unabridged

M
MASTERS

ULVERSCROFT
Leicester

First published in Great Britain in 1997 by
Macmillan
an imprint of
Macmillan Publishers Limited
London

First Large Print Edition
published 1998
by arrangement with
Macmillan Publishers Limited
London

British Library CIP Data

Masters, Priscilla
   And none shall sleep.—Large print ed.—
   Ulverscroft large print series: mystery
   1. Piercy, Joanna (Fictitious character
   —Fiction 2. Policewomen—Fiction
   3. Detective and mystery stories
   4. Large type books
   I. Title
   823.9′14 [F]

   ISBN 0–7089–3955–4

Published by
F. A. Thorpe (Publishing) Ltd.
Anstey, Leicestershire
Set by Words & Graphics Ltd.
Anstey, Leicestershire
Printed and bound in Great Britain by
T. J. International Ltd., Padstow, Cornwall

This book is printed on acid-free paper

Author's Note

For the purposes of this book it became essential that the cottage hospital at Leek be capable of dealing with broken bones as well as other pathology.

They probably are anyway.

Prologue

It was his mother who first asked the question. He was playing in the garden, setting a trap for a tiny blue bird, a common little thing of no importance. Absorbed in the trail of seed that led towards the jaws of the pottery jar, he had not noticed her leaning against the door until she had spoken.

"Tony," she had said in a soft, sorrowful voice. "Do you feel no pity?"

At the time he had failed to understand her. It was only now — twenty years later — that he was able to answer her question.

Pity . . . feel pity? No. Never. He felt emotion, sometimes, as he had when the bird had not fallen victim to his plan but had escaped.

He knew anger.

He knew excitement, too . . . the planning stage. That was so exciting. Finding a way to approach his victim with all the cunning of the seed trail and the trap that would seal the bird inside. Yes. That was exciting. Luring the victim to a place of secrecy.

Watching the panic — the terror in their faces — the realization that they were about

1

to die. Sometimes he allowed them to pray. If they were good Catholics he allowed them to beg for absolution. Perhaps that was pity.

He knew contempt, too. And this job had inspired that.

The contempt was for people's meanness. They were happy to hire him. Yes . . . His Roman lip curled. They wanted him to do their dirty work for them. But when it came to paying, that was a different matter. Didn't they understand the skill as well as the planning that went into these jobs? No cheetah stalking a zebra ever used more skill, more stealth, more cunning. And yet his most recent . . . His eyes flashed at the recollection.

"So much money for a moment's work?"

He had struggled to hold back his temper. "A moment? You do not understand? I spend many days thinking about the best way to deal with this matter, choosing the place, the time." His voice had toughened. This was the way to deal with clients. "I — am — a — professional."

1

She watched him slit open the letter with curiosity.

"Jonathan . . . ?" She glanced anxiously across the breakfast table. "Jonathan," she repeated.

He was staring at the piece of paper in his hand. She herself had handed it to him, noted the neatly typed address, the white envelope. But it had evoked no apprehension. Instead she had felt thankful that it was not another bill. And so she had given it to him, unconcerned, the past forgotten. She had carried on buttering her toast before reaching for the marmalade jar. Then she had looked up and noticed her husband's white face.

"Jonathan?" she said again.

He held the letter at arm's length, his face drawn and tired, each line heavily marked in grey.

Confounded, she reached out and took it. "Not the police again," she said, and he shook his head, worked his finger around his collar to try to loosen its stranglehold.

Still calm, she slipped on her bifocals and

3

peered down through the half-moon. It took only a moment to read the letter. One sentence, short and to the point. She flicked over it twice before giving a brief laugh. "Some sort of advertising stunt? Well, they've picked on the wrong one here, haven't they?"

Jonathan Selkirk closed his pale eyes and with some effort opened them again while his wife watched him, puzzled.

"I mean, surely it's some clever trick — isn't it?" She stopped, held her hands out. "What else could it be?"

"Advertising stunt?" He stared at the page in her hand. "You think it's an advertising stunt?" He looked angry. "You silly woman. If it's advertising, where's the name of the firm?" His breath came in quick, dry whistles. "You honestly think they'd send some sort of crappy circular about making a will — to a solicitor? I always knew you didn't have two brain cells to rub together. You have to be one of the most ignorant, most stupid women."

His wife took this unexpectedly coolly. She took her glasses off, folded and rested them, lens uppermost, on the table. "There's no need to be quite so rude, Jonathan," she said levelly. "Advertising isn't always obvious, you know. It can be quite subtle."

She glanced at the letter again before smiling and dropping it back on to the table. "My advice is to ignore it. Put it in the bin."

He glared at her. "Is it indeed?" he said. "To ignore it?"

His wife nodded.

"Perhaps you're right." His voice was hoarse.

The couple continued with their breakfast, she filling her mouth with toast while he slowly sipped his tea, until his gaze drifted back to the sheet of paper.

"But it is a threat, you know." He appeared to be having real trouble breathing now. "It's a threat," he repeated. "And I have a good idea who's behind it."

His wife concentrated on chewing her toast before speaking again. "Who do you think is behind it, Jonathan?"

"You know."

"I wonder." She tapped her chin rapidly with her index finger while her husband watched, irritated.

"Oh, you can't mean them. Now who's being silly — and paranoid? That was years ago. It's all forgotten. Forgotten and forgiven."

"Huh." Jonathan Selkirk made an ugly face. "The stupid are often thought of as naive," he said. "Neither forgotten nor forgiven, Sheila. People like that have long memories, full of sentimentality." He gasped. "They're the type who use such clichés . . . Long sins have long shadows — and rubbish like that."

His wife stood up. "No," she said. Then her fine, dark eyes seemed to soften. "I'm sure you're wrong. But these sentimental, stupid people seem to have upset you. You don't look very well." She smiled again. "You should be treating this letter as a joke."

Jonathan's face was plum-coloured now. "A joke!" he exploded. "A joke? This . . . " He slammed his outstretched hand down on the paper. "This is no joke," he said. "It is not meant to make me laugh — but *fear*." His face was contorted with pain now.

★ ★ ★

Detective Inspector Piercy felt the vibration behind her as the lorry approached. She steered her bike as close to the kerb as she dared and kept her head down, bracing herself against the inevitable turbulence. The noise was deafening and she felt dwarfed by the lorry's immense bulk. It was approaching fast, almost level now, poised to swing out

6

and overtake. It started to move past. And as she glanced over her right shoulder her eyes were drawn in to the massive tyres spinning as though they threw out a magnetic field. She crouched lower over her handlebars.

What happened next was sudden and quick. And it gave her no warning. Something on the lorry must have touched her and thrown her off balance. She was hurled from her bike into something hard and heavy. She heard a crack, a smash as her bike made impact. A searing pain in her arm. Then she lay, panting and winded, intolerable hurt darting through her body, especially her arm.

She remained still on the verge, disbelieving, the lorry disappearing into the distance in a haze of exhaust.

"Bastard!" she screamed. "Bastard." She raged futilely. He hadn't even known she was hurt. He'd felt no impact, heard no sound. He would arrive safely at his destination unaware of the collision. While she . . . She glanced along the road, both ways. It was empty. Still early. No one had seen the accident. No one would report it, act as witness, stop and help her, call for an ambulance, pick the bike up. And it was this that forced her to sit up and inspect herself.

Her cycling shorts were torn and muddied, her legs bleeding. Her head hurt and her eyes felt puffed and strange, the road bulging in and out of focus. And she felt sick and shaky.

It was her right arm that had taken the full impact. Now it was numb. But the sharp angle of the wrist to the arm told her it was broken. And later on — when the shock had lessened — she knew it would hurt.

She struggled to focus on the road but it was still swinging away from her. She looked at her bike. It was a mess too. Buckled wheels, bent handlebars.

She took a deep breath in, battled with her tears, dropped her head into her arms. "Shit."

Then she tried to stand up. Immediately the scene spun like an old-fashioned roundabout . . . out of time, out of focus, out of vision. And so she sat, uselessly, by the side of the road, still feeling dizzy and sick until a car skidded to a halt and a man climbed out.

"Come off your bike, duck?" he said. "Hurt, are you?"

She bit back every single sarcastic retort and merely shook her head. Then she fainted.

"Jonathan," she said, "are you all right?"

Her husband's face was an unhealthy grey. "Of course I'm not all right," he snapped. "I've got that blasted pain again. Get my pills. Quickly."

His eyes closed wearily. He knew he was a sick man. He needed peace and quiet — a cooling touch, loving care. He struggled to get his breath. Sheila — if only he were free of her. Through the pain he smiled. He had plans. But . . . His face darkened and he picked up the letter. It had been written on a word processor on a sheet of pure white A4, best-quality typing paper. And it was short, consisting of only one sentence. Unsigned, undated, with no address at the top.

'JONATHAN SELKIRK,' it said simply and in capital letters. 'MAKE YOUR WILL.'

★ ★ ★

Vague dreams of ambulance sirens screaming, people asking her if she could hear.

"What's your name, love?"

"Joanna," she mumbled.

"Have you right as rain in a jiffy," a cheery voice assured her.

9

And someone else told her not to worry — twice.

She didn't until another voice, brisk and businesslike, asked who was her next of kin.

The feeling was returning to her arm. Her guess had been right. It did hurt. She tried to move it and found it heavy, immobile and useless. She peered down at it. They had wrapped it up in a massive blue inflatable splint.

She gave up.

★ ★ ★

Jonathan had melted as many tablets under his tongue as the doctor allowed, but the pain got steadily worse. His wife watched his lips turn blue before she made her decision.

"I'm going to ring the doctor," she said firmly. "This isn't like your other attacks."

He gave her an evil glance. "Leave the quack out of this, Sheila," he said. "Nothing he can do except more bloody pills." He tried to stand up. The pain dropped him back into the chair.

"I'll be all right," he protested. "Don't fuss." He glared at her, catching his breath with the pain. "I'm not a helpless child."

She bent over him. "But, Jonathan,"

she said sweetly. "I really think you may be having a heart attack. You've had warnings enough. Maybe you've had your last warning."

He looked up at her, the expression in his cold, pebble eyes changing to one of fear.

"Warnings enough? Last warning?"

She smiled. "I mean the angina, dear." Her face was close to his, her eyes bold and staring. "Whatever did you think I meant?"

Jonathan Selkirk glanced back at the letter. "You'd like that, wouldn't you, Sheila?" he said suddenly. "A heart attack would do very nicely, wouldn't it?"

She ignored the comment until she'd found the doctor's telephone number in their personal directory. Then, as she waited for the phone to be picked up, she turned and looked at him, her face still pleasantly smiling. "Now don't be silly, Jonathan," she said calmly, a mother scolding a fretful child. "Of course a heart attack wouldn't do — not at all." Then she turned her attention back to the telephone. "Ah — Dr Matthews . . . It's Sheila Selkirk here. I'm afraid my husband's . . . "

The rest of the day's post lay unopened on the breakfast table, forgotten.

* * *

11

Efficiency, bright lights, stinging antiseptic. A bright bottle of clear fluid that somehow led into her arm and made it feel cold, her neck stiff and rigid in a splint, her cycling helmet off, someone slicing through her frayed shorts with a pair of scissors. She tried to protest and a nurse told her it was the only way.

"Something for the pain, dear." And a bee sting in the side of her leg. She swallowed. Her mouth felt dry.

A tall man in a dark suit swam into vision. He told her what she already knew — that her arm was broken — and that they would have to operate. Then mercifully she went to sleep.

★ ★ ★

The doctor took one look at Jonathan and rapped out a couple of questions. "Pain?"

Jonathan nodded.

"Where? Up the arm?"

For a second time Jonathan nodded.

The doctor picked up the bottle of pills. "How many of these did you take?"

"Six."

"Have they helped?"

"No."

The doctor turned his attention back to Sheila. "He'll have to go in. He's probably

12

had a heart attack." He looked accusingly at her. "Worry, stress, overwork. I did warn you." He picked up the telephone and ordered an ambulance.

Sheila Selkirk was agitated. "Not hospital, doctor," she objected.

The doctor's hand slid across the mouthpiece. "We've no choice, Mrs Selkirk," he said. "He needs rest . . . complete freedom from stress."

"Not hospital." This time it was Jonathan who was objecting.

"Just the cottage hospital," the doctor decided. "We can keep an eye on you there."

Husband and wife seemed satisfied.

★ ★ ★

Someone in white was sitting on her bed. She opened one eye and mumbled, "Matthew?"

He was watching her with an expression that churned her vulnerable stomach. He gave her a grave smile, leaned across and kissed her forehead.

"Jo," he said. "You gave me such a fright."

She closed her eyes and swam away. "I'm sorry."

Men in white coats. She rarely saw Matthew in his. In the mortuary he always wore

13

theatre greens. Theatre greens . . . sounded like a vegetable . . . She dreamed and felt his hand touch her unplastered one.

* * *

On the floor directly beneath, Jonathan Selkirk was trying to get rid of his wife.

"There's absolutely no need for you to stay. The nurses can look after me." He was watching her pack his clothes in a small, overnight case.

"I'll take these home, dear."

"There's no need for you to stay," he repeated. "I wish you'd go and leave me alone. Please go," he added irritably.

"I'll go," she said, "very soon." She gave him a strange, hurt look. "You'll be free of me before long. I'll come again this evening — see how you are. Well, I'll be off." She smiled. "Things to arrange. I must ring the office and tell them."

"Don't bother. I'll do it."

She bent over him. "Remember what the doctor said? Complete freedom from stress."

She was back again that evening, staying too long, moving around the bed and studying the machines he was wired up to. "I wonder what they all mean," she said idly, "what good that does." She looked at the bottle of clear fluid leading into his forearm.

Her husband stared balefully at the TV monitor. "And how am I supposed to get any sleep with that thing bleeping away all night?"

His wife twiddled with the knobs. "I understand you only have to worry if the alarm thing goes off."

Sure enough the machine emitted a high-pitched scream and one of the nurses came running in. She took one look at her patient, turned the knob to terminate the noise and gave Sheila Selkirk a severe stare. "Please," she said, "don't touch anything. They're all set."

Sheila watched her go. "I suppose," she said, "that they're all life-savers in one way or another."

Something passed across Jonathan's face — a shadow . . . tension and apprehension. And he felt uncomfortably aware of his wife's presence, of her restless movements around the room, of her touch.

At last she did go. She gave him a dry kiss on the cheek.

"Goodbye, my dear," she said very softly. "I'll see you later."

It was only after she had carefully closed

the door behind her that he realized she had taken all his clothes and left only his pyjamas, slippers and a dressing gown. He was imprisoned here. He pressed his buzzer and asked the nurse to wheel in the telephone. The nurse looked dubious. She muttered something about complete rest.

"The telephone!" he barked.

But the nurse left. He was alone.

* * *

Outside her husband's room Sheila Selkirk was speaking to one of the nurses.

"It was a heart attack," she insisted, "wasn't it? The doctor did say. It *was* a heart attack." She tightened her grip on the black canvas bag.

The nurse looked at her, puzzled. "We can't be absolutely sure . . . Not just yet." She paused. "By tomorrow we should know."

Sheila Selkirk nodded. "By tomorrow?"

The nurse put her hand on Sheila's arm. "Of course," she soothed. "We just want to be absolutely sure. There's no need for you to worry."

Sheila's face grew hard. "I'm not worried," she said.

The nurse gave a warm smile. "They all say that."

16

Sheila stared at her.

"The first twenty-four hours," the nurse said. "Once they're over that they're almost always OK."

"Quite," Sheila said and she turned and walked up the corridor. "Not that way," the nurse called after her. "It's the other way to get out."

"But . . . ?" Sheila Selkirk pointed to the exit sign.

"Just a fire exit," the nurse explained.

★ ★ ★

Matthew was still there when she opened her eyes again. But he had moved. Now he was standing with his back to her, staring out of the window. She lay without stirring and watched the movement of his square shoulders and the light, tousled hair. She rarely had the chance to study him undetected, standing still, not knowing she was watching him. So she indulged herself and lay, watching him quietly from beneath drooped lids, and hoped he would turn around before she slid off to sleep again.

He did. He cleared his throat, ran his fingers impatiently through his hair and turned around to see her.

"You're awake," he said, smiling. He

17

stood, staring at her for a moment, then crossed the room in two long strides, bent and kissed her forehead. "Like Sleeping Beauty," he said, laughing. "You've been asleep for hours. It's late, almost nine o'clock." He cleared his throat and sat down on the edge of the bed. "I've done a full day's work and come back."

She smiled lazily, dropped her good arm around his neck. "And you still smell of antiseptic, Matthew."

He took a deep breath. "They've put a pin in your arm. It'll be sore and you'll have the plaster on for a few weeks." He gave a tentative smile. "I sneaked a look at your X-rays. I thought you'd want to know."

She glanced at the plastered arm. "I knew it was broken straight away — without an X-ray."

He grinned at her. "All right, smarty-pants. What you didn't know is that it was a bit of a bad break. You managed to break both bones. Jo," he said softly, "you were lucky it wasn't anything worse. What exactly happened?"

A quick flashback to the lorry, wheels spinning, pulling her in. "I think I got snarled up in the wheel of a juggernaut."

His eyes were warm, shining green but quite serious. "Then thank God you're all right. How will you manage on your own?"

She struggled to sit up. "What do you mean?"

He looked around the room. "Cooking, washing. You won't even be able to drive. And certainly not cycle," he added severely.

"Mike can pick me up."

"You won't be able to work," he said. "You need looking after."

Her face hardened. "No, Matthew," she said. "I'll manage — somehow."

He gave a long sigh.

"*I'll manage*," she repeated. "I'll be all right."

He sat quietly on the edge of the bed for a long time, staring at her. She found his hand and squeezed it.

"I will manage," she repeated firmly.

He gave a quick exclamation of annoyance and an angry frown. "I thought you'd say that." He paused. "You could move in with me," he said diffidently. "There's plenty of room and I could look after you."

She dropped back on the pillows. "I don't think so," she said. "I'm not ready for that."

Matthew's lips tightened. "Be reasonable, Jo," he said.

"I'll *manage*," she said, fiercely this time.

"We'll see." Matthew sighed as he bent

over her and kissed her cheek, stroked her hair away from her eyes.

"How's my bike?"

He made a face. "A wreck. But I did get the bike shop to pick it up. They seem to think they can make it rideable again."

"Good." She smiled lazily.

"Now let the nice nursey give you an injection. Go back to sleep, Joanna," he said. "I'll pop in and talk to you first thing in the morning. Before I start work."

He paused at the doorway. "Please think about what I've said. The offer's there." His eyes rested on her affectionately. "Now is as good a time as any."

He grinned self-consciously. "Besides, I've always fancied myself as a nursemaid."

If she'd been feeling better she would have given him an earful. As it was she closed her eyes and drifted off almost immediately.

* * *

In the room below, Jonathan Selkirk watched the corridor light dancing along the ceiling.

2

Through the night her dreams were confused and disturbing. She dreamt that Matthew was offering her a small, brass key, which she took and cradled in her palm. It was warm . . . then it grew hot and hotter still, and when she looked down she saw that it had burned right through her hand, leaving a hole the shape of a key. She peered through the hole and saw the spinning wheels of the lorry, changing patterns like the view through a child's kaleidoscope. Next she was lying in the middle of the road, clutching her arm and screaming while a car sped towards her. She was unable to see the driver's face from where she lay.

At some time in the night she woke with a dry mouth and rang her bell. Through the dark a nurse in white moved and spoke softly, asking if she was in pain. She swallowed the cold, crystal water and sank back on the pillows. Then she slept and when she opened her eyes the room was filled with early-morning sunshine and someone was standing at the foot of her bed, watching her.

She struggled to focus. Matthew had said he would drop by in the morning. But it wasn't Matthew who was standing there, it was Sergeant Mike Korpanski. She stared at the broad shoulders and dark hair and frowned. "Bit early for sick visiting, isn't it?"

"Sorry about your accident," he said awkwardly.

She narrowed her eyes and studied his face. He was scowling, his dark eyes avoiding hers. His shoulders were tensed. She knew Mike. This was how he looked when he had a problem and judging by the grim expression on his face his problem was not a small one.

"Mike," she said. "What's going on?" She tried to sit up. "What is it? What are you doing here?"

He watched her without speaking, still scowling. And now she became aware of other things in the background. There seemed to be increased activity around the ward, doors opening and shutting, voices — loud voices. All strange noises for a hospital. She lay back against the pillow and waited for him to speak.

But being Mike his explanation was both violent and unexpected. He moved away from the bed, banged his fist down on the windowsill and glared at her.

"Why of all times why did you have to come off your bloody bike yesterday?"

"Mike," she said patiently. "I didn't elect to get knocked down. It just happened. Now are you going to tell me what's going on or am I supposed to play twenty questions?"

In the background she heard the unmistakable wail of a police siren moving closer. It stopped outside the hospital.

Mike took two steps towards the bed. "Last night someone — a patient — disappeared from his hospital bed." He stopped. "We think, I mean . . . " he shuffled awkwardly. "He could have wandered off. We don't know. We're not sure. But it looks as though someone could have taken him from his bed."

"Him?"

"A man," he said. "A middle-aged solicitor, admitted yesterday with chest pain. Heart attack. His bed was found empty this morning."

Joanna frowned at him. "People do leave hospital," she said slowly, "for all sorts of reasons." She listened again to the noises foreign to a normal hospital day. "So why do you say he was abducted?"

"He was wired up to all sorts of machines, with a drip going into his arm. The wires

23

had been yanked off really hard. There were bits of skin and hair still sticking to the plasters."

She looked curiously at him. "And?"

"There were drops of blood all the way to the fire door. The doctor thinks it was from where he'd pulled the drip line out." He paused. "But surely if he was just legging it out of the hospital the obvious thing would have been to press on it and stop it bleeding? I mean, he wouldn't just let it bleed — or would he?"

Joanna nibbled her fingernail. "So where did he go?"

"He seems to have disappeared into thin air. There's no sign of him anywhere and he was only wearing his pyjamas."

She moved her plastered arm. "I take it you've searched the immediate hospital grounds as well as his home?"

Mike moved two steps closer and frowned. "Joanna," he said. "What's the anaesthetic done to your brain? We've already looked in all the obvious places. I came here hoping for inspiration. Ideas. Not some bloody lecture you'd give to new constables the first day on the job." He paused. "This was an ill man, very ill according to the doctor. They really did think he might have had a heart attack." His hand was clenched in a fist. "I think someone may have ripped him off those machines and taken him from the hospital — against his will."

"Surely they have hospital security?"

Mike gave an expression of disgust. "A couple of half-blind porters in their seventies. Doors and windows open everywhere."

"Was this man's room on the ground floor?"

Mike nodded. "And the room next door to him was empty with the window wide open. So anyone could have got in."

"No one saw him go?"

"No."

"What does his wife say?"

Mike tapped his lip thoughtfully. "She doesn't seem too upset. She's convinced he'll turn up — somewhere."

"But there's no sign of him?"

Mike shook his head. "He really has disappeared, Jo. I'm sorry, I shouldn't have said anything." He stole a glance at her arm. "Colclough would be furious if he knew I'd even mentioned it. He's convinced you have major injuries and won't be fit to work for months. Forget it," he said, now eyeing the plaster cast with undisguised hostility. "That thing'll take weeks to heal. I'm sure we'll have found him by then." He aimed a kick at the foot of the bed. "Dead or alive."

But already the adrenalin was coursing through her veins. It dissolved the pain, gave her energy, made the mummy shape of her arm nothing but a bulky nuisance. She sat bolt upright.

"Who was he?" she asked. "What was his name?"

Mike smiled grimly. "Was, Joanna? Was? Jumping to conclusions? After all you've said to me about being impulsive."

"Well, that's what you think, isn't it?"

She looked closer at him. "You think he's dead, don't you, Mike?"

"You do," he accused.

"Yes," she said slowly. "I do. Yet," she mused, "I wouldn't have called myself a pessimist. And people do get stressed in hospitals — do strange things. Sometimes they wander off." She frowned. "But the circumstances are unusual, aren't they? You say the IV line and machines had all been turned off?"

He nodded.

Her curiosity was alight now. "Tell me more about him."

Mike sank into the chair. "His name is Jonathan Selkirk," he said. "He's a solicitor here, in Leek. He specializes in criminal law."

A sudden image of a hard-eyed, humourless

man with a toothbrush moustache edged into her memory. "I know him," she said. "Sly old Selkirk and that crooked partner of his." She looked at Mike. "What's his name?"

"Wilde. Rufus Wilde."

She closed her eyes and struggled with something. "Aren't they under investigation? Fraud Squad job?"

"That was months ago. I haven't heard anything about that for ages. Solicitors," he said disgustedly. "Some of them are more bloody crooked than half the villains they're defending."

"That's a bit of a sweeping statement, Sergeant. Most of the solicitors want justice every bit as much as we do."

"It depends on your interpretation of justice," Mike said darkly.

Joanna moved her plaster cast across the sheet. It felt cold, heavy, unfamiliar. Inside it her arm ached. "Let's not get into prolonged discussions, Mike. Is there anything else I should know about Selkirk?"

"Now hang on a minute," he said quickly. "You're off sick. I just came to pick your brains."

"Really?" And even Mike knew she was laughing at him.

He paused before shrugging and adding, "OK, I admit it. I mean you've only got

27

a broken arm haven't you. His wife did mention something about him receiving a letter through the post yesterday morning. She thought it could have triggered off his heart attack."

Joanna looked up. "What sort of letter?"

"It advised him to make a will."

And Joanna jumped to exactly the some conclusion that Sheila Selkirk had jumped to only the day before. "It was probably just a circular," she said, "or Make a Will Week. I'm always getting letters advising me to make a will."

But Mike shook his head. "No," he said. "It was a typewritten note which told him to make a will, and it rattled him. I've seen it. There wasn't a letterhead, a telephone number or anything to get back to. No." He shook his head firmly. "It wasn't advertising — nothing to do with that. But it wasn't your regular threatening letter either."

"Then what sort of letter was it?" Joanna asked sharply.

"I don't know. It was addressed to him and told him to make a will. That's all."

"So what did you think the point was, Mike, if it wasn't advertising?"

"A warning?"

She looked up. "A *warning*?"

"Well . . . you know." He stopped. "It

could have been a sort of death threat."

"And now he's disappeared?" Joanna thought for a minute. "I don't suppose his wife has any idea who sent the note?"

Mike shook his head. "Not that she was going to tell me anyway. All I got from her was that it had a local postmark. She thinks he'll turn up."

"But you think he's been kidnapped."

Mike protested. "I didn't say that."

"Well, what else does 'taken against his will' mean?" She pushed on. "You think he's being held somewhere — or that he's dead." She spoke the words flatly, as a statement.

Mike paused, then said, "I could do with you, Jo. I'd like to find him — soon."

It was the nearest she would ever get to Mike begging.

"Send the nurse in," she said. "I'm getting dressed."

★ ★ ★

There was a formality of signing a form . . . a disclaimer, absolving the hospital of any blame. And she knew they disapproved. She ignored it. Mike was right. He needed her. Besides, she wanted to find Selkirk too. So she signed the form then sat and waited while he organized a WPC to fetch some clothes from home. Something she could easily slip on. And all the time she waited she was in a fume. Intrigued and impatient.

When the WPC returned Joanna knew why Matthew had known it would be necessary for her to have help. She was disabled by the plaster cast, much more than she had realized, unable even to pull up her knickers properly.

She looked hopelessly at the WPC. "PC Critchlow — Dawn," she said. "You're going to have to help me."

The WPC giggled. "I'd guessed that," she said. "You're not going to get very far with all your clothes lopsided like that. And that thing on your arm."

"A necessary evil, I'm afraid."

Even in her impatience Joanna was forced to smile at her reflection. Her skirt was crooked, her tights twisted, her sweater half-on, half-off. She was helpless, her progress irritatingly slow. But even what progress she was making was suddenly brought to a halt by Matthew bursting in, still dressed in his theatre garb.

"Joanna . . . " He scowled. "What the hell's going on? I heard you were discharging yourself." He glowered at the WPC who flushed and muttered that she would wait outside.

Matthew watched her go with taut impatience before he turned back. "Now, would you mind explaining?"

She smiled. "Not at all," she said, "if you'll just give me a hand with my sweater."

He cleared his throat before helping her wriggle her good arm through the sleeve and tucking the rest around her.

"Thank you," she said, ignoring his angry glance. "You were right, it is a bit tricky."

"Told you it would be. Now what's going on?"

"A patient went missing from here last night."

Matthew dismissed it with a wave of his hand. "It was some old fool with hospital phobia," he said. "I heard about it. It's hardly enough to get you from your bed. Joanna," he said softly. "You could do with the rest. It was a nasty bump. You were concussed, you know."

"I'm all right now, Matthew," she said. "Please, don't fuss. I'll seek medical advice if I feel ill. A man's disappeared. And they need me. I can co-ordinate things — direct the others." She stopped. "It's not as though I have to do all the footwork."

"You need the rest," he repeated angrily. "They can manage without you."

"You know how much work there is?" she

31

said frowning. "They can't manage this sort of major investigation on their own. They need everyone they can get. Not someone off sick."

He gripped her shoulders. "He's just some silly old fool," he said. "Probably lost his memory . . . wandering the streets. He'll turn up."

"Mike told me all his wires had been ripped off," Joanna insisted. "He told me there was blood on the bed. It had dripped all over the floor." She paused. "I don't think even a silly old fool would have done that. And if he's simply wandering the streets dressed in a pair of pyjamas why hasn't he turned up, been found by someone?"

Matthew glared at her. "It's all you bloody well care about," he said. "Law and order and your beloved police force. Think you're Joan of Arc, crusading for right against wrong."

She hated him for that and was glad when he stormed out.

★ ★ ★

It was easy to find the missing man's room. The bright tape across the doorway, the army of Scene of Crime Officers in their white suits, the curious stares of staff and patients dawdling past. She slipped on some overshoes and went in.

Mike was standing at the foot of the bed, directing operations. For a moment she watched him. The scene was still one of chaos and confusion when order should by now have set in. In the centre of the room, surrounded by medical machines, was the bed, a narrow, high hospital bed with a small wooden headboard, labelled Jonathan Selkirk, date of birth 24.3.40, and presumably the consultant's name. A Mr Meredith. The sheets had been thrown back and the bed was strewn with a tangle of multi-coloured plastic-coated wires, still attached to a blank television screen. But the other ends — the ends she supposed had been attached to the missing patient — terminated in small squares of sticking plaster. She bent over and saw hairs and pieces of skin still attached. Mike had been right. They had been torn off and dropped across the bed.

"Make sure you get pictures of this lot, will you," she said to the camera man," and then cut the ends off, bag and label them, and get them to the lab."

She turned her attention to the far side of the bed. A tall steel stand was holding a bag of clear fluid, the pipe leading to the bed and ending in a tiny plastic tube. It must once have been taped to Selkirk's arm. Now it led to a puddle, mixed blood and the clear fluid. And blood was splattered across the floor in large drops. Joanna glanced at the sticking plaster on the small plastic pipe and saw that it too was smothered in hairs and flakes of skin. It must have been pulled out with some force. No gentle hand here. She looked around her. They were all watching her with confident expectancy.

She stood still for a moment and studied the room. Even crawling with police there was something ghostly about it, abruptly robbed of its occupant. The blank monitor which should have showed the beat of his heart, the drip apparatus that should have led to his vein, the empty space where he should be lying, the pillow dented by his head and still displaying a few stray grey hairs. Only one thing was missing — Selkirk himself. And she knew why Mike had been anxious to find him.

She looked up. "Best check the staff's fingerprints," she said, "and be thorough with the room. Check it as carefully as if he were lying here dead." They all involuntarily glanced at the bed as though they expected his corpse to materialize. "If he turns up," she added, "we'll scale down operations."

She caught Dawn Critchlow's gaze. "You'd

better tell the ward sister the room's out of bounds for at least forty-eight hours."

WPC Critchlow disappeared and the others all set to their various jobs.

Mike grinned. "Joanna," he said, glancing at her plaster. "Are you going to be all right?"

"Fine, with the help of the maximum legal dose of aspirin and some decent coffee." She glanced back at the stiff, dried blood.

"The doctor said the drip must have been torn out," he said. "Switched off at the clip, then pulled. Some blood would naturally have drained." He swallowed. "The nurse discovered the patient missing then found drops of blood all the way to the fire exit. Frightened the living daylights out of her."

"He used the fire exit," she mused. "So that's how he got out without being seen?"

Mike nodded.

"The nurse's name?"

"Yolande Prince," Mike said. "She's very upset."

"Mmm. I'm sure. I shall want to speak to her." She glanced at one of the PCs standing by. "Make sure she's available as well as the other nurses on duty."

"At the station, ma'am?"

"No, here will do. I think they've probably

had enough shocks for one day," she added drily.

She stared at the bed then back at Mike. "What did you say he was wearing," she asked curiously.

"Pyjamas."

"Just pyjamas?"

Mike nodded and indicated the hook on the back of the door. "His dressing gown's still here," he said. "And . . . " He bent down and picked up a pair of brown tartan slippers. "We found a couple of footprints along the corridor. He was barefooted."

"I wonder why he didn't bother to put his slippers on."

Mike looked at her. "That's another reason why I thought he'd been abducted rather than simply left. Even suicides aren't keen on cold feet. It's automatic to put footwear on."

She stared at the floor. "He came in yesterday — dressed?"

"His wife took all his clothes home," Mike said. "We asked her."

Joanna nodded. "How did you think someone might have got in?"

"Next door," Mike said. "There's an empty room."

"Ah yes," she remembered. "With an open window." She glanced at Mike. "A bit opportune, don't you think? Did you look on the sill?" she asked. "Are there any marks?"

Mike shook his head.

"Well get the SOCOs to scrutinize it anyway." She crossed the room and looked out of the window to the small turning space outside. "And then what?"

"Sorry?"

"Well, Selkirk's left the hospital, either alone, contemplating suicide or with somebody, possibly under duress. Then what? You say you've searched the grounds and he isn't there. So how did he get away? Walking or by car?"

Mike swallowed. "I don't know," he said frankly. "I hadn't thought that far ahead."

"Well, let's take a look outside," she said, nodding to the SOC team. "Carry on. And don't forget to photograph all of the blood stains. And get samples of each one." She paused. "Just on the offchance that one of the splashes isn't his."

They nodded, gave a swift smirk at her plaster, and carried on with their work.

The trail of blood drips was easy to follow — straight to the fire door, as Mike had said. And there was a bloody smear at hand height.

Joanna studied it for a moment.

Mike nodded. "They've already photo-graphed it," he said, "and lifted some prints. I'd take the whole thing off, only it's a hospital door. And right now," he added, "he's just a missing person."

The fingerprints were clear. "Looks as though he pushed hard against it," she said. "Very hard for such an ill man."

"Unless *he* was pushed."

She frowned. "It's a strange case," she said. "Abducted, from a hospital. Why?"

Mike chewed his thumb. "I don't know, Jo," he said. "I was hoping you might have some bright ideas."

She shook her head. "Not yet." She stared again at the door. "And what are these prints?"

A grained mark was discernible about four inches above the handprint.

Mike shrugged his shoulders. "I don't know," he said. "I hadn't worked that one out — yet."

"But it's bloody too. If someone left using this door they just might have got in this way too."

They walked through the doorway and crossed a flagstone path leading to a row of parking spaces. Joanna sighed. "I suppose the fire door wasn't locked." She sighed.

Mike shook his head. "Fire doors," he

said. "Regulations. No, they weren't locked because they can only be opened from the inside."

"So security was lax . . . and he could easily have left in a car."

"Yeah."

"Who's his next of kin?"

"Wife," Mike said, "and he has a son."

"Just the one?"

Mike nodded.

"Anything else there? A mistress, perhaps?"

He paused. "Not so far. Come on, Jo. He only disappeared a few hours ago."

She allowed herself a slight smile. "Yes." The parking spaces had been taped off. "Get this inspected, Mike, then let the cars in. Otherwise all the side roads will be blocked with staff cars. You know how short parking spaces are."

"OK."

"You've had a preliminary look out here?"

"Nothing," he said gloomily. "He just disappeared into thin air."

"So what happened to the spots of blood?"

"They end at the car park."

Heads bent, they followed the blood. Clear to see on the flagstones and darker even than the black tarmac of the car park.

"So someone brought a car up and he got in."

"Or was bundled in," Mike said.

"Did anyone see anything — hear anything?"

"Not that we've found so far."

"How?" she said. "If it was suicide how did he get the car to come here for him? Was it a friend's car or was it a taxi? But if he was depressed or worried about something and wanted to kill himself . . . " She looked back at the foreboding brick walls of the old-fashioned Victorian hospital, "Why not do it here? Why leave the hospital? Was someone in cahoots with him?" She looked at Mike. "If not his wife, did a friend come and pick him up in his car, take him home? And I suppose the one name that springs to mind is Wilde . . . Rufus Wilde . . . his partner. But" she said, "if someone did forcibly abduct him against his will, why from here when it would have been a lot easier grabbing him from home or work? So many people are milling around a hospital. Day and night. And there's a much greater chance of his being spotted by someone."

She shrugged her shoulders and turned back towards the door. "Well," she said. "I'll have a word with the nurse first. What did you say her name was?"

"Yolande. Yolande Prince. I'll find her for you."

"Mike." She sighed. Her arm was hurting

now, and felt heavy. "Mike, when I've finished with Yolande Prince will you drive me to Selkirk's house? I want to talk to his wife."

He grinned and nodded. "But of course. Your chauffeur, ma'am."

She watched his bulky shape stride along the corridor and disappear through the far door, then studied the tall building. A hospital should be a sanctuary. One should be safe here because if not here, then where?

3

Staff Nurse Yolande Prince was a large girl with frank, blue eyes and well cut short dark hair. She looked pale and tired from the ordeal of the previous night and gave a sharp yawn as she sat down. Immediately she smothered her mouth. "Gosh," she said. "I am sorry. It's been an awful night, just awful." A shadow crossed her face and she stared at the floor. "Sometimes I think I'm jinxed."

Mike cleared his throat. "We just want to ask you a few questions," he said. "Then you can go to bed and sleep."

But the strain of the previous night was catching up with the nurse. She stared straight at Joanna, her face ashen and haggard. "I'll probably be in big trouble about this," she said, "but I'm sure you'll find him. He's all right, you know." She looked from one to the other. "It'll be memory loss — or something."

"Just tell me about last night, Yolande," Joanna said sharply. Her arm hurt and it was making her fractious. She wanted some strong coffee — and a couple of aspirins.

"You came on duty — at what time?"

"Eight o'clock." The nurse frowned. "There were supposed to be four of us," she complained. "Two teams of two looking after the patients. But bloody Robbie . . . " She looked even more annoyed. "He was off sick." She glared at Joanna. "Maybe if he hadn't, Mr Selkirk wouldn't have taken himself off."

Joanna was quick to latch on. "Is that what you think happened?"

Yolande blinked. "Well, what else? No one would have walked in and dragged him off. He'd have shouted, wouldn't he?"

Mike gave Joanna a swift glance.

"We don't know what happened yet, Yolande," Joanna said testily. "We don't want to guess. At the moment we're simply fact-finding." She smiled at the exhausted nurse. "And we hope, too, that Mr Selkirk will turn up safe and well with nothing worse than memory loss." She didn't add that this seemed unlikely.

"Let's get back to last night, shall we? There were three of you on duty?"

Yolande nodded. "It made things very difficult," she carried on. "There were eighteen patients and some of them were quite ill." She glanced desperately at Mike. "There just wasn't the time to keep a close check on him."

43

Joanna leaned forward. "Tell me, Yolande, how ill was Jonathan Selkirk?"

The nurse looked puzzled. "What do you mean?"

"Was he, for instance, confused? Depressed?"

The word seemed to have an effect on the nurse. She looked, panic-struck, from one to the other. "I can't say," she began with difficulty. "I can't say about depression . . . No, not depression," and she closed her eyes wearily. "Although," she looked up, "he was a bit down. Well, you would be, wouldn't you, if you'd had a heart attack?"

"Of course. Of course . . . " Both were quick to reassure the nurse.

Joanna decided to drop the issue of depression. "Let me put it another way. Did he seem as though he wanted to get out of hospital — go home, perhaps?"

Nurse Prince shook her head. "No," she said. "Not really."

"Did he seem worried about anything?"

"I don't know." Yolande scowled. "I don't. Really, I don't. I hadn't met him before. Perhaps he always seemed worried about things."

"Had he had a heart attack?"

"Oh yes," she said. "Almost certainly." She stopped. "His ECG was normal, and so was his blood pressure. But he looked a pretty awful colour. And I could tell he was feeling rotten."

"You spoke to him?"

The nurse nodded. "And to his wife, before she left."

"At what time?"

"When I was giving out the night drugs," she said. "Round about nine."

"What exactly did Mr Selkirk say to you?"

"He said he had some pain, and I asked him if he wanted an injection."

Joanna glanced at Mike. Surely an injection would have made him drowsy? "Did he have one?"

"No. He said he could manage." She stopped for a moment, thinking. "Perhaps he wouldn't have gone if he had had an injection. It would have made him too sleepy. Maybe it *was* my fault."

"Was he supposed to have one?"

The nurse shook her head. "Oh no. Only if he had asked for one."

"Did he say anything else?"

She thought for a moment. "Yes," she said. "He asked me for the telephone."

Joanna pricked up her ears. "Did you bring it?"

"No. We were really busy. I just didn't have the time."

"Perhaps one of the other nurses?"

Nurse Prince shrugged her shoulders. "I'm sorry, I really don't know. You'll have to ask them."

Joanna let the subject drop. She could pick it up later with the other two.

"At what time did you last see him?"

"Well," she began, embarrassed, "we were supposed to be looking in on him every hour."

Joanna rubbed her aching fingers. "Look," she said. "I'm not the night sister. I don't care what you were supposed to do. It doesn't matter to me. If it helps, I have an idea you were extra busy. But it's important I get the facts straight. We have to know how long Mr Selkirk could have been missing before his empty bed was discovered. All right?"

But the nurse didn't look reassured by this. She looked even more worried.

"I feel awful about this," she said, "responsible." Her hands were pressed together, shaking. "It's almost as though I was jinxed. Last year — "

"Stick to the point, please," Mike interrupted. "We want to know what's happened to Jonathan Selkirk. That's all. We just want to find him, love."

"I checked him at eleven," Yolande said

46

slowly. "All his observations were fine. He was almost asleep. I asked him if the pain had gone and he said yes, he was feeling much better but very tired." She stopped. "I closed the door." She looked defensively at Joanna. "He needed rest. He was tired. The ward was noisy. He wouldn't have got much sleep with the door open. I wished him a good night and closed the door. I . . . I didn't see him again."

"What happened next?"

"At about four I thought I'd better check up on him. I was just going to check his pulse, blood pressure . . . I opened his door . . . " She thought for a moment. "It was ajar. I assumed one of the other nurses must have been in."

"And had they?"

Yolande shook her head miserably. "They thought I'd been keeping an eye on him."

"What else can you remember?"

"The overhead light was on. The bed clothes were thrown back." She looked at Joanna. "You saw the leads. They'd been torn off. And he'd pulled his drip out." She stopped and her face seemed to crumple. "I panicked. Shouted for the other nurses. I hoped he'd be in the loo." She was gnawing her thumbnail. "We searched the whole ward — absolutely everywhere." She gave a brave attempt at a smile. "Even the cupboards. Then Gaynor saw the blood on the floor."

She looked helplessly at Joanna and some of the panic of the night reached the two detectives. "We followed the blood spots all the way to the fire door. We used a torch and saw they led outside. Then I rang Night Sister. The porters hunted outside the hospital as far as they could." She stopped. Her eyes were wide and frightened and it was clear the memory of this night would stay with Yolande Prince. "We were calling his name really loudly. After about half an hour Sister rang the police. They were here really quickly," she finished helpfully.

Mike nodded. "The call was logged in at six o'clock. They were here within ten minutes."

"That's all I know," the nurse said, "except that all this plus last year will probably cost me my job. And it isn't my fault."

She stood up then. "Is that all?" She gave another huge yawn and this time didn't even bother to try to disguise it. "I really am whacked."

"Just two more minutes," Joanna said.

Mike shot Joanna a quick glance and made the sign of a tilting cup before giving a deliberate glance at her plaster cast.

She looked gratefully at him. "And a

48

couple of aspirin, Mike," she said, before turning her attention back to the nurse.

"The room next to Mr Selkirk's."

The girl's hand flew up to her face. "What about it?"

"Was the window left open?"

"Yes," she said emphatically. "It was."

Joanna watched her carefully as she asked the next questions. "So someone could have climbed in through the window and got to Mr Selkirk's room without your knowing?"

Dumbly, Yolande Prince moved her head up and down.

"Did you hear a car during the night?"

The nurse thought for a moment before nodding. "Yes," she said. "When I was on my way back from my lunch. It was around one."

"Can you tell us anything about it?"

"No," she said frowning "Not really. It sort of pulled up and stopped. I thought it was one of the nurses being dropped off. He left the engine running." She smiled. "I just thought someone was having a goodnight kiss."

"Did you look out of the window?"

Yolande shook her head. "I walked on to the ward and chatted to the other two."

"Did you hear the car move off?"

"I can't remember," she said. "A car's

just a background noise. No one takes much notice, unless it's doing something odd, you know . . . noisy or terribly fast."

Joanna nodded. It was not a step forward but neither was it a step back. She made a mental note. They'd better check none of the nurses was dropped off in the car park at around one a.m. If none had, this might be the vehicle they were looking for.

Mike returned balancing two cups and slipped her a couple of tablets. "Courtesy of Sister," he said.

Joanna swallowed them down with a swig of machine-made coffee and thought for a minute. "What time did his wife leave?"

Nurse Prince thought for a moment before answering. "Around nine," she said, "as far as I can remember. I spoke to her as she left. She was heading for the wrong door."

Mike shot Joanna a swift glance.

The nurse continued. "She tried to leave . . . " The significance of what she was saying suddenly registered. "I didn't mean . . . "

"She tried to leave through the fire door?"

Yolande nodded dumbly. "I expect she was glad to leave," she said after an awkward pause, then flushed. She looked miserable. "I'm always saying the wrong thing. What I mean was that some people — have a problem with being in hospital — take it out on their relatives."

She smiled. "You know what I mean?"

"No, not really." Joanna was in an uncompromising mood. "Do you mean Jonathan Selkirk was unpleasant to his wife?"

"More than that. He was rude." She looked at the floor. "He wasn't a nice man." She met Joanna's eyes almost defiantly. "We don't have to like our patients, you know, but . . . " She passed her hand across her brow. "I feel so responsible. He was ill and he was my patient. I feel really guilty."

"OK, Yolande," Joanna said finally. "You can go home now, to bed."

There was no doubting the relief on the nurse's face.

When the door had closed behind her Joanna turned to Mike. "Get the other two nurses on duty that night interviewed, will you? One of the PCs can do it. I'll talk to them later. Ask them to concentrate on the basics, times, anything seen, anyone say anything. Perhaps they can find out whether Selkirk actually did use the phone. Ouch."

She winced as a sharp pain travelled up her fingers along her arm. "I want to get out of here. Take me round to his house, Mike. I'd like to meet his wife."

51

She stood up and looked around the shabby room with its bare floors and flaking paint, a huge, oak desk in the centre smothered with stacks of papers. The cottage hospital was a strange mix of vintage NHS and modern science. A computer stood in the centre of the desk, three green telephones side by side, silent now.

Mike crossed to the window and spread his meaty hands across the radiator. He stared out across the car park and the neat lawns. "I wonder where he is," he said. "I wonder how he left without anyone hearing him. If he was taken, why from here?" He turned around. "The whole thing is so . . . " He fumbled for the right word and as usual couldn't find it. "So unnecessary."

"Well, we aren't short of possibilities," she said. "A mistress, a boyfriend, a haven, the old memory loss." She laughed. "A sudden brain storm . . . Depression." Her mood changed suddenly. "Or maybe he had an enemy. Then again we might never find him. We might never know the answers to any of your questions. He might join the rank and file of the Missing Persons Register. Who knows?"

A sudden mood of depression washed over her. Perhaps it was a combination of delayed shock from her accident — or the

52

anaesthetic. Or even the realization that even in hospital one might not be safe if someone wished you harm.

* * *

The Selkirks' house was beautiful, authentic Georgian red brick with neat white paintwork, a pillared portico and pleasing symmetry. The drive was gravelled and free of weeds and the borders neat and still colourful.

Mike drew the car to a halt then walked round to open the passenger door. "And don't expect this sort of fancy treatment to carry on once you're out of plaster," he warned.

She grinned and thanked him.

The door was flung open and a big, handsome woman in a floral dress with bright auburn hair crunched across the gravel towards them. "Have you found him yet?" She had a deep, booming voice and sounded angry as though a child were playing truant from school. Angry, Joanna noted, not worried, and she scrutinized the woman's face. It was heavily lined and deeply sunburned. Joanna could picture her crewing on a sailing dinghy somewhere hot with a relentless sun beating down. Perhaps it was the heartiness, the strength behind the firm, deep voice, the heavy, rolling walk in inappropriately smart patent shoes.

"Mrs Selkirk?"

The woman eyed her plaster cast with suspicion.

"I'm Detective Inspector Piercy," Joanna said. "I think you've already met Detective Sergeant Korpanski."

The woman nodded. "Have you found Jonathan yet?" she repeated impatiently.

"I'm sorry. Nothing so far. But we're working on it. I've abandoned my sick bed to look into the disappearance of your husband, Mrs Selkirk," Joanna felt compelled to add. "We are concerned."

"Oh dear," Sheila Selkirk said without a trace of sympathy. "I am sorry."

"Do you think we could come in?"

The three of them crossed the drive, watched by a huge golden retriever who gave one loud bark. When it was ignored it went back to sleep again. Sheila Selkirk touched the dog with her foot. "Bloody useless hound," she said. "Wouldn't protect us from Charles Manson. No aggression," she complained as she led them into a square, cold sitting room, devoid of ornaments.

"Mrs Selkirk," Joanna began with difficulty.

54

"As I'm sure you can appreciate, any number of things may have happened to your husband."

"I'm not daft," Sheila Selkirk barked. "I've got a bloody good imagination, Inspector."

"Yes," she said quietly. "So please help us by answering all of our questions as frankly as you can."

Joanna looked again at the woman's face. A thick layer of make-up, bright lipsticked mouth, furtive dark eyes. A strong personality?

"To your knowledge, Mrs Selkirk, did your husband have somewhere he might have gone to?"

The woman's eyes gleamed with intelligence. "Do you mean a mistress, Inspector?" Her mouth twisted with a strange humour.

Joanna shrugged. "Possibly."

Sheila Selkirk wiped mascara-stained tears from her cheeks. "God, no," she said, laughing. "Sex hardly featured in my husband's life." She smeared another black trickle along her cheek and laughed again. "He had a job getting it up on our ruddy honeymoon, Inspector. And that was years ago when he was a young man and relatively virile. My husband," she said, "is now late into middle age. So you might try the traditional prerogative of middle-aged men.

Not sex . . . my dear, a nubile, warm-blooded female."

Mike was shuffling his feet.

"Menfriends?" Joanna asked delicately.

"Again, no." This time her voice was firm and without humour. "My husband was not a homosexual and he had few close friends. I have already telephoned them all." She paused. "Except his partner."

Mike raised his eyebrows and Joanna caught his glance and nodded before turning her attention back to Sheila Selkirk.

"Was your husband depressed?"

This time Sheila Selkirk nodded. "Yes," she said frankly. "He was depressed. I think severely so." She paused. "He refused to acknowledge it, of course, or to see a doctor about it. But then that's the sort of person my husband was."

"Was?"

"Now come along, Inspector." Sheila Selkirk's voice was firm, schoolmarmish, bordering on being patronizing. "Is — was? Don't let's pretend. My husband is a very sick man. He was admitted yesterday with a suspected heart attack. Wired up to dozens of machines. I know he was also very depressed and had talked to me of suicide." She stopped and drew in a long, deep breath. "I had done all I could to persuade him to consult his

GP. He took absolutely no notice of my advice." She looked coolly at Joanna. "What else could I do? At least I assumed he was safe when he was admitted to hospital. But then in the middle of the night he pulls out his tubes, rips the wires off and disappears, leaving behind a trail of blood. Now what am I supposed to think? At first I was convinced he'd turn up. But as time moves on I wonder. If you ask me he's topped himself," she said unexpectedly.

"I beg your pardon?" Joanna was shocked, more so than if Sheila Selkirk had used the f-word.

"The trail of blood stopped at the car park," Mike said. "We believe someone must have met him there, given him a lift. Who?"

Sheila Selkirk shrugged her shoulders. "A taxi? Or . . . " She paused. "He might have bound the wound up and stopped the bleeding."

"He wasn't even wearing his slippers." Joanna glanced at Mike. His bulky shoulders were tensed, like an animal's, ready to spring. His gaze at Mrs Selkirk was frankly hostile.

"It wasn't you, was it, Mrs Selkirk, who picked him up?"

Sheila Selkirk glared at him. "I was with a friend all evening."

"His name?"

Sheila Selkirk looked angry. "Just what are you implying?"

"Nothing," Joanna said frankly. "We're implying nothing. This is all purely routine," she said, "just like ninety-nine per cent of all police work — boring, pointless questions which don't lead us anywhere." Her pupils were tiny, hard pinpoints. "But we still ask them, all the same."

"I was with an old family friend," Mrs Selkirk said crossly. "Someone both Jonathan and I have known for years."

"His name," Mike said woodenly.

"Anthony," Mrs Selkirk said. "Anthony Pritchard. Not that it's any of your bloody business. He's an old family friend. Quite innocent."

"As you said." Mike was giving her no points. "Innocent family friend." He paused. "Married, is he?"

She sucked in her breath and spat out the answer. "Widower. His wife and I were very close friends. She died tragically of cancer five years ago."

"I see." Mike always managed to sound offensive in situations like this.

Joanna felt it was time to step in. "Was there anything your husband was particularly depressed about, Mrs Selkirk?"

Jonathan Selkirk's wife blinked and she sat very upright on the sofa. "Well, things aren't terribly brilliant financially. People don't pay when they ought to. Damned bloody legal aid and no money around these days."

Joanna thought for a minute, then asked almost casually, "What exactly did your husband do?"

"He was a solicitor. Don't you know *that much*, Inspector?"

"I know he was a solicitor, Mrs Selkirk." Joanna felt quite angry and her arm was beginning to ache again. The effect of the aspirins must be wearing off.

"What I meant was, what branch of the law did he specialize in?"

"Criminal law," Sheila Selkirk barked without apology. "His job was to defend the little prats who go around breaking the law. That's what he did for a living. Mostly legal aid work," she added. "That was his bread and butter. Unfortunately at about the same time as the government withdrew about half the funding for legal aid they put up the cost of living." She stopped and a veil dropped over her eyes. "Hence the trouble paying the wretched bills. And then your lot . . . " she glared at Mike, "decided to give him some hassle over a few paltry claims."

"Ah," Joanna said. "You mean the Fraud

Squad investigation."

"Fraud!" Sheila exclaimed. "Absolutely bloody ridiculous." She scratched the side of her mouth. "But a worry all the same."

Mike's eyes were fixed on the woman's face without a trace of sympathy.

"Poor old Jonathan," Sheila Selkirk continued. "All this trouble . . . worry. He'd suffered from angina for years. Then he gets that bloody letter."

"Ah yes," Joanna said. "The letter."

"Yesterday, in the post. Wait a minute . . ." She stood up. "I'll go and fetch it."

The skirt of her dress rustled as she moved swiftly towards the door. Joanna glanced at Mike. He screwed up his face and she knew he disliked Sheila Selkirk. But she didn't. Yes, the woman had a powerful personality. Some might call her overbearing. But there was an honesty, a directness, that Joanna felt she could relate to.

She was back in a minute, tossed the letter towards Joanna. It floated free for a second before landing on her lap. Joanna read it twice without touching it, then looked up.

"At first I thought it was advertising," Sheila Selkirk barked. "Jonathan took it as a rather pathetic threat."

"And who would threaten your husband?"

"Solicitors meet all sorts of people."

It was a vague, evasive reply.

"Whatever it meant, we were both disturbed by it."

Mike was studying it over her shoulder. "I should think you were, Mrs Selkirk." He stared at her. "And had he?"

"Sorry?"

"Made a will."

She took a deep breath in. "My husband is a solicitor, Sergeant Korpanski." A touch of humour lightened her face and they could both see that once — not very long ago — Mrs Sheila Selkirk had been a very handsome woman. "What do you think? He'd actually made several, I believe." Then she looked thoughtfully at him. "Tell me, Sergeant," she said, "are you naturally that shape or do you have to work at it?"

Mike spluttered and Joanna smothered a silent giggle. She loved to see Mike baited. Sheila Selkirk was perceptive enough to know that Mike disliked her. And this was her revenge.

Joanna turned her attention back to Jonathan Selkirk's wife. "May I keep this?"

"Do what you bloody well like with it."

"Thank you." Joanna paused. "And had your husband ever received a letter like this before?"

"Absolutely not."

So again Joanna changed tack. "Do you think it is possible, or probable, that someone abducted your husband from the hospital? Possibly even for money?"

Sheila Selkirk gave another explosive laugh. "You mean kidnapped?" she said. "For a ransom . . . Jonathan? Oh, my dear. They'd wait a long time for their money." Her face was pink with humour. "Kidnappers don't target middle-aged criminal solicitors. They go for pink-cheeked sweet little babies. Worth far more money, don't you think?"

Then she leaned towards Joanna, revealing an eyeful of ample cleavage. "Are you married, my dear?" She chuckled again before adding, "It wouldn't be worth their while kidnapping Jonathan . . . I wouldn't pay the ransom, even if I had the money. And where's the demand, eh? Where is it?"

This time it was Joanna who was discomfited. For all her honesty and directness, Sheila Selkirk was an embarrassing woman. So she ignored the comment.

"Tell me, Mrs Selkirk," she said smoothly. "Is there *nowhere* your husband might have taken refuge, away from the hospital, if he was depressed or unhappy? If not close friends, your son, perhaps?"

Immediately the words were spoken she knew the dart had pierced a sensitive spot.

Sheila Selkirk flushed. "You know about him, then? My son . . . " Sheila Selkirk drew in a large, deliberate breath. "You know about Justin?"

"I know only that you have a son." Joanna's curiosity was pricking her.

Sheila Selkirk's face seemed to crumple. "Yes, I have a son," she said sadly. "His name's Justin." Here she stopped and stared out of the window, at the browns, reds and golds of the autumn trees. Her breath came in slow, heaving gasps. "Unfortunately he and Jonathan . . . " she cleared her throat noisily, "they didn't get on. They never have. In fact," she swallowed, "it would be nearer the truth to say that they couldn't stand the sight of each other. Jonathan packed the poor little blighter off to boarding school the minute it was considered decent." She turned her gaze back to Joanna. "I don't really think Justin ever quite forgave him. He was bullied rather mercilessly." She closed her eyes in pain. "Kids, they can be so cruel. Far more cruel than adults, you know."

And a picture of Eloise flashed across Joanna's mind. "Yes," she said softly. "Kids can be cruel, more cruel than . . . "

Sheila Selkirk seemed not to notice. But Mike was more vigilant. He shot her a sharp, enquiring look and for once Joanna met his eyes and didn't even try concealing her feelings.

Sheila Selkirk started. She looked at them both. "Funny," she said drily. "Isn't it? His own flesh and blood and they just hated each other. In fact, Inspector," she said calmly now and without emotion, "if one walked into the room the other would walk straight out. They skirted round each other, avoided one another. The school holidays were sheer misery for poor old Justin. Absolute misery. And Jonathan did everything he possibly could to avoid coming home."

"Where does your son live now?"

"Here, in Leek." Sheila Selkirk stared boldly at Mike. "He's a teacher in the so-called Special School, the one for the children we would once have called retarded or mental defectives. They have some silly name for them now — severe learning disabilities or some such nonsense." She grimaced. "All that expensive education, Sergeant. Public schools cost a fortune. And my son ends up teaching a bunch of morons." Her dark eyes fixed on Mike. "No justice, is there?"

"Is he married?" Mike chipped in.

Sheila nodded. "Oh yes." And then unexpectedly her face softened and again her strange beauty shone through. "He has a daughter," she said. "A lovely, lovely little thing." She flushed. "Oh dear, here I am, boastful grandma . . . But she really is a dear little thing." She gave a short, self-conscious laugh. "Three years old. Wait, here . . . " She crossed the room to a small, mahogany chest of drawers. It was so packed with photographs that she had difficulty opening it. She leafed through them until her hands touched one and she handed it to Joanna. It was a picture of a Shirley Temple lookalike . . . a laughing, curly-haired, beautiful child, plump cheeks and dimples.

Sheila Selkirk gloated over it, her mouth quivering and moist. "Lovely, isn't she? Look at those eyes, her mouth, her beautiful little curls — exactly like Justin's at the same age."

She took the photograph from Joanna's fingers and stared straight at her. Unhappiness tightened her face into spasm. "I suppose you're wondering why the pictures are stuffed into an already over-full drawer." She closed her eyes in sudden, tight pain. "Unfortunately, Jonathan's dislike of his son extends even to our granddaughter." She gave the picture a fierce stare. "He wouldn't have a photograph of little Lucy in the house at all." She gave a sideways glance at the chest of drawers and laughed. "Had he been a slightly more curious man," she said, "he probably would have found these pictures." She stopped and the look of anguish was blended into one of fury. "And then he would have burnt them," she said lightly.

Joanna and Mike looked at one another.

"I'm sorry, Mrs Selkirk," Joanna said gently, steering the conversation back on course, "do you have a photograph of your husband?"

The woman looked up sharply. "What for?"

"Identification," Mike said. "Someone might have seen him."

"Sergeant," Sheila Selkirk said coquettishly. "When my husband disappeared last night he was wearing a pair of brown and cream striped pyjamas and bugger all else. I should think if he's wandering up and down Leek High Street someone would have called in a couple of your strong-arm colleagues." The idea seemed to amuse her thoroughly.

"A photograph, please, Mrs Selkirk."

She recovered herself quickly. "Somewhere," she said.

Joanna and Mike both gave an involuntary glance at the drawer.

"Not here," she said. "I don't put their photographs together." She smiled and disappeared from the room, returning a few minutes later with a studio portrait of a grave-looking middle-aged man without a trace of humour in his face. She looked down at it for a moment, then handed it to Joanna. "This is my husband."

★ ★ ★

"Well," Joanna said as Mike took the car down the drive. "So far, apart from the nurse who's only worried her head may roll, we seem the only ones at all upset by the man's disappearance."

Mike grinned. "Look on the bright side, Jo," he said. "She could have been one of those really neurotic tyes, breathing down your neck all hours of the day and night. At least like this she'll keep off our backs until we find him."

She turned her head and stared at him. "Dead or alive, Mike?"

"Well," he said. "He was too sick a man to be wandering the streets for thirty-six hours in nothing but a pair of pyjamas. The weather's quite cold. If he hasn't taken refuge with a friend he's quickly stiffening."

She smiled at him. "Thank you, Mike,"

she said, "for your usual graphic and dispassionate thesis. Now commit yourself, Sergeant. Dead or alive?"

"Dead," he said soberly, "and some poor bugger's got to find him."

4

She kept the preliminary briefing short, emphasizing the point that so far Jonathan Selkirk was a 'missing person with cause for concern'. But as the hours ticked by, all the listeners were homing in on the same thought. The search would probably end with a sodden body, a crumpled heap of extinguished life.

She mentioned the probability that a car had picked him up and knew she could rely on a couple of them to check along the taxi rank as well as among his circle of friends. True, Sheila Selkirk had already rung their close friends, but it was possible that though Jonathan Selkirk's whereabouts had not been revealed to his wife, they might be to the police. Joanna's years in the police force had taught her to rely on no one's statement until it had been thoroughly checked.

After the briefing Mike drove her home. She watched him handling the car with a touch of peevishness, irritated that the plaster cast was slowing her down, forcing her to be dependent. Making an invalid of her.

"He asked for the telephone," she said.

"I wonder who he wanted to phone. His wife?"

Mike took his eyes off the road for a moment. "She claimed she was out all evening with her innocent family friend."

"Since when have you started believing alibis?"

"Just reminding you," he said good naturedly. "Surely it's more likely that he wanted to ring for a taxi?"

"Ripped all his wires off and climbed in wearing pyjamas?" She shook her head. "Even taxi drivers have their suspicions."

"Maybe he had a bag of clothes with him."

She shook her head again. "His wife took the only bag of stuff away with her."

"As far as we know."

"From what she and the hospital staff have said, he wasn't in a fit state that morning to be packing bags of clothes."

Mike agreed.

"Anyway, thanks for the lift," she said as he pulled up outside her cottage.

"My pleasure. I'll be along in the morning — nice and early."

"You're at the gym tonight?"

He grinned and flexed his muscles.

"You should have told Sheila Selkirk how she could get a body like yours."

"See you tomorrow," he said, and she laughed as she slammed the car door behind her.

Even getting her keys out of her bag was tricky. Turning the key while holding down the door handle was even worse. Elbows have no grip. And her damaged arm had no strength either. She cursed softly and eventually opened the door. Inside, she struggled feebly with her jacket. The sleeve was too tight over the plaster and it tore.

"Damn," she cursed softly and wondered whether she should have accepted Matthew's offer and moved in with him. But she knew it would be easier to move in than to move out. She filled the kettle awkwardly and sat, pondering, before hunger drove her back into the kitchen.

Matthew arrived at eight thirty, a take-away tucked under his arm. He grinned at Joanna and held out the brown paper carrier bag. "This is a large slice of humble pie," he said, bending and kissing her cheek. "I'm so sorry."

He gave one of his boyish, apologetic grins and rubbed his chin ruefully.

"The only thing I can say in mitigation is that I really did think it would be better for you to have a couple of days' rest instead of charging around the place on the hunt for a missing patient."

"If this is Chinese humble pie," she said, sniffing the contents of the bag, "you're forgiven."

"It is," he said. "And I'm sorry. I didn't really mean you were like Joan of Arc."

She met his eyes. But in anger there was an element of truth.

He smiled and drew her to him. "My mother always told me the way to a woman's heart was through her stomach," he said softly, into her hair.

"Your mother," she said, "sounds a remarkably sensible woman."

He tilted her chin towards him and stared at her. "You should meet her."

"Should I?"

Matthew drew back and hung up his jacket. She didn't pursue the subject.

"Well, as I didn't think you were going to manage much in the way of culinary adventures with that thing on your arm . . . " He was speaking too quickly, "I thought . . . "

Sometimes she wondered whether Matthew's parents would ever accept her. Perhaps not while he had a daughter and a legally bound wife. Occasionally she would wonder which of the three disliked her most?

Like Snow White's stepmother peeping

72

into the magic mirror, the answer never varied. Eloise hated her most and the answer still had the power to wound her. Maybe one day she would cease to care but today, already wounded, it still did.

She walked into the kitchen and picked up two plates with her good hand.

Matthew's voice reached her there. "I remember when Eloise broke her arm . . . "

The kitchen seemed suddenly icy, frost edging under the door, through the windowframes, down the stairs. And even Matthew, with his selective, wilful blindness, must have sensed it as she returned with the plates.

" . . . anyway, she couldn't do anything for herself," he finished quickly. "I only hope your help with the investigation was worth leaving that luxurious hospital bed for. Besides all that delicious free hospital food."

She motioned towards the food. "Nothing as good as this."

"Well," he said as she set the plates awkwardly on the table, "have you found the old goat yet?" He clutched his chest and staggered around the room. "Lost — man with chest pain wearing pyjamas." He shot a wicked glance at her. "And did I hear he was dripping blood?"

73

She laughed uneasily. "Theatrical, — isn't it?"

"Just a bit. Surely the whole case is quite simple," he said. "Just follow the blood trail." He gave her a mocking glance. "And you a Detective Inspector, Joanna. Really."

She enjoyed sparring. "It ends in the car park."

"So," Matthew said in conspiratorial tones, "an accomplice with a car."

She shrugged.

"What do you think — was he loopy or depressed? Or possibly both?"

"I honestly don't know about his mental state," she said, "and we haven't found him in spite of the police search."

She paused for a moment before adding, "His wife's not exactly concerned about his disappearance." She put her head on one side, considering. "And that always makes me a bit uncomfortable, when the next of kin are less concerned at a disappearance than are the police. In fact," she said, forking stir-fry into her mouth, "I cast her more as the merry widow than the grieving one."

Matthew looked up. "You do think he's dead, then?"

She shook soy sauce over the food. "Where else could he be? He isn't at home. It doesn't seem that he had many friends. His son, by his wife's account, hated him. He was a sick man. The nights have been cold and he was only wearing pyjamas. We think he's been abducted." She paused. "We've a few lines of enquiry. The car he left the hospital in, and there's a possibility he made a phone call." She sighed. "Obviously he might not have actually spoken to anyone. But assuming he did it could have been either a colleague or a taxi firm. There are always unanswered questions. Sometimes even after the end of a case. I only hope we get the answers to some of them. And then there's the tiny matter of finding the body." She grinned at him. "Just to provide you with a bit of work. We'll intensify the search of open wasteland, rivers and the canal tomorrow."

"Well," he said, pouring them both a glass of wine, "if no one else is bothered about him, why are you so concerned?"

"It's my job, Matthew. Besides . . . " she considered for a moment and looked at him, "I have a very strange feeling about this case. It's so atypical. So many unusual ingredients." She stopped. "And there's another reason you definitely won't understand."

He moved closer. "Try me."

"Well," she began, then stopped. "It's really silly."

"Go on."

"Well," she said again, slowly. "We spent part of last night under the same roof. We shared a house. We were both in hospital. The same one." Then she caught sight of his face. "You don't understand, do you?"

He laughed. "In a way," he said and she left it at that.

They ate in silence for a while.

"I thought people weren't supposed to speak ill of the dead," she said suddenly.

"You mean the wife?"

"Yes."

"Well, maybe she doesn't think he's dead." She shook her head.

He looked at her. "What did she say that caused you such offence?"

"I tried to suggest he might have a mistress. She replied he couldn't even get it up during his honeymoon. Horrible, isn't it?"

The room fell silent while Matthew turned his wine glass around in his hand and stared moodily into the ruby glints. "And when are *we* going to have a honeymoon?" He asked the question lightly, in his habitual bantering tone, but when she glanced at him he'd stopped looking into the glass as though it was a crystal ball and his eyes were resting on her. Their expression was quite cold.

For once she had no flippant answer for

him. Nothing to deflect his question. So she sat miserably and they ate the rest of their food chatting desultorily, the atmosphere destroyed. He changed the subject back to the safe area by asking her what she thought the chances were of finding Jonathan Selkirk still alive.

"Well, as I said, we think he was abducted. Mike's a hundred per cent sure he was, and I'm inclined to agree with him."

Matthew made a face. "Don't tell me Tarzan's actually said something clever for once."

"Oh, Matthew," she said reproachfully. "Behave. Mike's been driving me around like a model chauffeur all day. And I agree with him. I think he's right and that Selkirk's dead," she said. "I also think nobody will cry many tears for him. He was not a nice man."

Joanna told him about the family photographs stuffed into the drawer and that Jonathan Selkirk had disliked his son so much he had refused not only to have his photograph around the house but even that of his three-year-old granddaughter. "And she looks quite a sweet little thing," she said.

"Didn't think kids were much in your line, Joanna." There was a tinge of dry sarcasm in

Matthew's voice that again chilled her.

She felt bound to say something. "Kids aren't 'in my line'," she retorted, "but this was Selkirk's granddaughter."

Matthew nodded. "I wonder why," he mused.

She looked at him. "Why what?"

"I wonder why he disliked his son so much."

She chased the last scraps of prawn cracker around her plate thoughtfully. "There's lots of reasons why people don't take to their offspring," she said at length. "Sometimes they suspect the child isn't theirs, sometimes they're jealous. Sometimes the kid is a little too like themselves — you know — it mirrors all their weaknesses. And sometimes kids are just horrible."

Neither of them mentioned Eloise. In fact, during the year since Matthew had left Jane, Eloise had quickly become a taboo subject. Matthew disappeared every other weekend and she knew he was taking his daughter out. But she was rarely mentioned because every time her name cropped up they argued. Matthew made occasional conscious efforts to remind Joanna that he had a daughter but it merely made the hair at the back of her neck prickle. Guilt — at robbing the child of her full-time father? Or was it more closely linked to Eloise's Identikit resemblance to her mother?

Matthew tidied the meal away, loaded the dishes into the dishwasher and they settled back to finish the wine. It was eleven o'clock when he reached across and touched her plastered arm. "I think now is as good a time as any," he said quietly. "Perhaps your accident has pushed us towards a watershed."

She already knew exactly what he was about to say.

"Why don't you sell here," he said, glancing round the cottage, "and move in with me? When my divorce comes through we can buy somewhere decent of our own."

His face was firm as he watched her. She knew he had already made up his mind and that the accident had merely precipitated the actual question. But she couldn't bring herself to speak. She loved Matthew — yes. But commitment? Her commitments were dual — both work and Matthew. And she had the uncomfortable feeling that commitment to the one might preclude the other.

She looked helplessly at him.

He moved closer, wrapped an arm around her shoulders. "Jo," he said, "it would be the best thing — for both of us. Please."

He stopped. "I mean, you *are* going to find it awfully difficult coping on your own. Your arm will be in plaster for a couple of months. Now is as good a time as any." His face was set and very firm. She knew Matthew well. Once his mind was made up he could be extremely stubborn.

"I love you, Jo." He spoke very softly, almost a whisper. But his eyes were unblinking.

She swallowed and her mouth was dry.

After a pause Matthew moved away. "I see," he said. "At least, I think I do."

So they sat awkwardly, and at midnight Matthew left. Back home to the top floor of the huge house he had rented from a friend for the last two years.

Joanna went to bed disheartened and depressed, but, thanks in part to the after-effects of the anaesthetic, slept like a log.

* * *

Mike hammered on the door just before eight and caught her still in her white towelling dressing gown.

She yawned and stretched. "Thanks for coming." And, to help hide his embarrassment, "For being so prompt and early you can make some coffee." He followed her into the cottage.

She was halfway up the stairs before she shouted down, "Anything turn up in the night?"

"Negative." She heard the kettle being filled. "But all the taxi drivers have been questioned. No one picked him up."

She did the best she could to wash and dress, clean her teeth and even managed a respectable smear of make-up. She settled herself across the table from Mike and drank the coffee.

"At the bottom of the canal," he said. "That's my bet. Maybe we should send a couple of divers down."

"Well, the nearest part of the canal to the hospital is four miles away so we can start there."

She was sitting in the car before he mentioned Matthew. "I nearly didn't come," he said. "I thought Levin might give you a lift in. I saw his car outside," he added.

"He left late last night." She shot him an angry glance. "Not that it's any of your bloody business."

They were silent for the rest of the journey.

★ ★ ★

Superintendent Arthur Colclough met them at the door, his jowls wobbling like an

81

excited bulldog's. "I've been trying to ring you," he said. "You'd better get out to Gallows Wood. Straight away. They've found something there."

"Selkirk?" they said in unison.

He nodded. "It looks like it."

★ ★ ★

Gallows Wood was a small wooded area on the edge of a new housing estate. Over the years it had given the police no more trouble than half a dozen other patches of waste ground close to the town. In other words, it was a haunt for alcoholics, runaways and courting couples. Lately the Staffordshire Wildlife Trust had taken an interest in the badger sett and had bought the small plot of land from the local council.

Joanna frowned at Mike as he switched on the engine. "I didn't expect him to have got there," she said. "It's a couple of miles from the hospital."

"So he must have got there by car."

"Wait a minute." She remembered something. "There's a footpath, isn't there? If you go round the back of the housing estate and cut across those old factories . . . " She frowned. "The question is, could he have stumbled, barefoot, about three-quarters of a mile across unlit, derelict ground, in his condition?"

Mike looked at her. "That might be the question. Let's just wait and find out." He switched on the blue light, pressed his right foot down to the floor and they reached the wood in five and a half minutes.

Two police cars were already parked, their lights still flashing. Mike pulled up behind them and spoke through the open window to the constable standing by.

"Which way?"

"In there," he said, pointing. "You have to go through the gate. Along the path. He's in the middle." He looked pale. Finding a body is a shocking business.

Joanna spoke to him. "Were you the one who found him?"

"Yes, ma'am."

"OK," she said. "Well done. The sooner he was found the better."

The constable nodded and Mike and Joanna climbed out of the car, looking around them. It was a pretty place, deserving of the Wildlife Trust's money, probably filled with birdsong throughout the summer days and badgers playing through the long, light evenings. But now it was dark and dripping as the sun disappeared behind thick grey cloud.

"Somehow," Joanna said, looking at the sopping leaves in the thick brambled undergrowth and the black path that twisted into its centre, "it looks the right sort of place."

"To top yourself? Yes," Mike agreed.

"Depressing, isn't it?" Joanna said as they scrambled through the gate. She glanced at Mike jumping over the stile. "Of all the things I find depressing it's a suicide." She took in a deep breath. "It's as though the whole of the human race has failed that person. And we're the ones who find them. It always makes me sad."

Mike attempted to cheer her up. "Well," he said. "He had a sense of humour. Gallows Wood. Ten guesses how he's done it."

She agreed.

They were wrong. On both counts.

★ ★ ★

Rain dropped heavily from the trees, splashing around them as they stepped through the undergrowth. Then suddenly the September sun emerged again to give the wood a pale, unreal light. It was a small wood, the path almost impenetrable with snarling brambles and soft, black mud.

Joanna glanced down at her shoes. "Bloody

mud," she said, "and with this thing on my arm they'll be tricky to get clean."

Mike turned round. "And I thought Levin licked your boots clean."

She stared at him.

It took them a couple more minutes to reach the clearing in the centre of the wood. They looked around them and knew this spot was completely hidden from both the road and the nearby housing estate.

The path turned sharply to the right and they saw the ring of police standing round a crumpled heap of old-fashioned striped pyjamas.

They pushed forward and Joanna caught her breath.

He was lying on his side, the back of his head clearly visible. His hair was cut short, making it easy to see the scorch mark of a bullet entry wound in the nape of his neck. His hands had been tied behind his back.

She knew what she would see even before she leaned across the dead man. He had no face. And she felt a sudden, shouting queasiness.

"Bloody hell," she murmured. And already she knew from the position in which he lay that he had had his hands bound and had been forced to kneel before the executioner's bullet in the back of his skull had killed him instantly. She forced herself to study him with a detective's eyes. Jonathan Selkirk lay wearing only pyjamas, feet bare, pathetically scratched and bleeding. A long black thorn stuck out of one of them. The back of one hand had continued to ooze long after the IV line had been removed, leaving a tiny pool of blood and a large bruise. And she knew whatever sort of man Jonathan Selkirk had been in life, he had done nothing to deserve this.

She addressed Mike over her shoulder. "Find out if they've contacted Matthew."

He grunted.

Others were arriving now, carrying police equipment. A plastic shelter was erected over the body and a walkway carefully taped off. Ten minutes later the photographer arrived, and, twenty minutes after that, Matthew. He made a beeline for Joanna.

"So you've found him," were the first words he said. "I'm glad," and, taking a step nearer and studying her face, "you look pale, I told you you shouldn't be working."

"Matthew, he was shot in the back of the neck." The words sounded cruel and cold.

Matthew gave a low whistle. "Shot," he said slowly. "I really didn't expect that."

"Neither did we." She gave a quick shiver. "It's made a mess of his head," she said.

Matthew shrugged. "I know," he said. "Guns are nasty things. They do a lot more damage than people realize. People think guns leave a neat little black hole. They just don't understand. One little bullet rips out a ton of flesh. Sorry," he added, looking at her now chalk-white face. "Darling, I'm sorry. Are you all right?"

She nodded. "His hands were tied behind his back," she murmured. "He was wearing the pyjamas he'd left the hospital in. No shoes." She swallowed. "There was a huge thorn sticking out of one of his feet. It must have hurt."

"Not half as much as what came next," he observed drily, looking beyond her to the crumpled figure. "Oh, I'm sorry . . . Sorry, sorry. I know. I've no sensitivity." He spat out the old joke. "That's why I'm a pathologist."

He knelt down by the figure and opened his black scene-of-crime bag to take out some gloves.

Matthew glanced around at the trees. "You'll find most of his brains around there," he said. "Be a good idea to take some specimens." Then he peered at the bullet entry wound. "I think," he said slowly, frowning, "at a guess a small handgun. But a lot of damage. More than I would have expected." He paused. "Professional-looking job, isn't it?"

Joanna stood quite still and knew Matthew had voiced what she'd been thinking. She glanced again at the dead man, then across at Mike. She knew he too had been thinking the same thing.

"I think I'll measure the calibre at the morgue." Matthew touched the bullet hole. "Get it more exactly. The barrel was jammed right against his head. Nice example of contact burn." He looked up at her. "I suppose there's no doubt it is Selkirk."

She nodded. "It looks like it." She smiled as she watched him work. "There can't be many middle-aged men wandering around Leek in nothing but a pair of pyjamas." She glanced at the back of the man's hand. "Especially men who've recently had a hospital drip pulled out."

Matthew turned his attention to the bindings on the wrists. He studied them for a moment before rolling the body over and staring at it for a while. Then he stood up.

"Judging from a very superficial examination, I'd say he most probably has been lying here since some time late Monday night/early Tuesday morning." He stopped. "In other words it's probable that he was brought from the hospital straight here and shot within an hour or so of the abduction."

He peeled off his gloves. "I'll be able to tell you more after the PM but I think we'd better get him formally identified first, if possible."

Her eyes were again drawn to the gaping face. "Identified?"

"Well, you know what I mean." Matthew addressed the photographer. "Finished? Fine. Then get him moved. I'll ring the Coroner, Joanna," he said. "And we'll do the PM this afternoon. OK with you?"

She nodded.

As the team were starting to move Selkirk's body Matthew touched Joanna's arm. "Jo," he said. "I don't know whether you've had time to think about this — started to draw any conclusions."

She could guess what he was about to say. "You think this is no ordinary killing, right?" Selkirk's body was being loaded on to the stretcher and covered with a sheet.

"No way," he said, shifting his weight from one foot to the other. "I don't exactly have experience of this sort of thing. But I've heard about them." He stopped. "It looks to me very like a professional job — an execution." He stopped. "A paid killing. The knots around the wrist — very deft and very firm. Someone visited the hospital that night. God knows why Selkirk didn't shout out. Why go meekly with an abductor?"

"If he had a gun held to his head?"

Matthew ran his fingers through his hair and gave her a worried look. "Maybe," he said. "Maybe. Anyway, as you've said, this person probably held a gun to his head, ripped all the electrodes off and pulled out his drip, bundled him into the car, drove him out here, at some time tied his wrists, forced him to kneel — and blew his face off."

She blinked at the brutality of his words yet knew he was almost certainly right. It had happened like this.

"But why? And who?"

He grinned at her. "That's where my work ends and yours begins," he said, "Darling."

5

"Let's get him formally identified first."

Joanna was sitting opposite Superintendent Arthur Colclough. Mike was propping up the door.

Colclough's plump face was sober. She had spared him none of the details. "I thought you said most of his face was missing?"

"Not quite all," she said shortly. "There's enough there, if we use our discretion with a sheet."

He nodded.

"I thought I might ask his son, save his wife the trauma."

Colclough grimaced. "But you said they weren't close. It shouldn't upset her, should it?" His nose was still in Joanna's preliminary report.

"Yes, but . . . " She left the comment to hang in the air. Colclough hadn't seen Jonathan Selkirk's body.

"That's what I like about you, Piercy," he said. "Always considering the victims' feelings." He leered at her. "I suppose you've thought of the fact that she's one of the chief suspects."

"So's the son," she said. "And if you think that not being allowed to hang her family portraits around the place is a just excuse for murder . . . "

"But how deep did it go?" Colclough wagged his finger at her. "That's what you've got to remember. How deep? She may have had this resentment festering for years. Something might have snapped. Or circumstances changed."

Joanna shook her head slowly. "You didn't see his body, sir. It didn't look like anything had snapped." She paused. "There wasn't a sign of anger or hatred. He'd been led there and shot in cold blood. It looked like a professional job. There was no beating up, no obvious bruises. Anyway," she continued, "we'll know more after the PM."

Colclough nodded. "So now what?"

She stood up. "I'm going over to the school where Justin Selkirk works to pick him up."

"He's a teacher?"

"Yes. In some sort of Special School."

"Right. How's the arm?" he asked kindly. "Not too sore, I hope?"

"A bloody nuisance. Still, Korpanski makes an able chauffeur."

Mike grunted and they both turned to look at him with amusement.

Colclough gave her a curt nod and she knew it was the nearest he would ever get to acknowledging her curtailed sick leave.

She was almost through the door when he called her back. "How professional, Piercy?"

"Sir?"

"How professional a job?"

"We'll know more after the PM," she said.

His eyes were grim and she knew he expected a better answer.

"It looked like a contract killing," she said reluctantly. "Even the knots were neat and tight."

★ ★ ★

A long, tidy curved drive led to the charming old house that was now the Tall Firs school for children with severe learning difficulties. A few vans were slewed across the entrance. Scaffolding was erected at the side of the building. As they approached, a workman shuffled past them, wheeling a barrowful of cement.

"I don't envy anyone the upkeep of this place," Joanna remarked.

Mike gave a twisted smile. "Think they appreciate all that's being done for them?"

She shrugged her shoulders.

"It's like the bloody old folks' homes," Mike continued sourly. "Palaces, most of them. And they're probably too knocked off to realize."

"Never mind, Mike," she said with a grin. "Maybe one day, if you play your cards right, you'll be lucky enough to end your days in a 'palace' like this." She turned and looked at him. "For goodness' sake, it's supposed to be the mark of civilized society how you treat your less fortunate members. Have a heart."

"I have," he protested. "I just don't like to see all my taxes going to waste."

She decided to tease. "Your wages come out of taxes, Mike. Some people might think that was a waste too."

"Score one-all," he growled. He pulled the car up outside the double glass doors and a tall woman immediately rushed out.

"Police," Joanna said, flashing her ID card. "We'd like a word with Mr Justin Selkirk."

"He's taking a class at the moment." The woman was polite but firm.

Mike stepped forward. "We can't wait," he said.

She looked him up and down. "Bad news?" she asked. "Have you found his father?"

Mike nodded.

"Then come with me. Please."

The noise echoed along the corridor, loud shrieks ... laughter, pain, terror? Neither could work out what it was apart from being a discordant cacophony.

The tall woman looked at them. "Singing," she said calmly. "It's part of their treatment. Tremendously therapeutic." She smiled enthusiastically. "They just love it."

Mike muttered something obscene under his breath.

They reached a scarred oak door with a wired glass window. The tall woman peered through it for a moment, then knocked and pushed it open.

There were about eight children sitting on the floor doing strange twisting movements with their hands, and screaming.

In the centre of the circle was a small, slim man with thinning hair. He too was knotting his hands, twisting his fingers, absorbed in the exercise. He wasn't screaming. But then he hadn't noticed the three visitors walk in.

"Mr Selkirk, Justin." The tall woman spoke sharply. "The police are here."

He stood up, alarmed, and lost balance, stumbling slightly. Around him the children were still making strange, strangled sounds and moving their fingers.

"My father," he said eagerly. "You've found him?"

Joanna nodded and wondered how this small man would cope with the ugly corpse they had lined up for him at the mortuary.

Justin Selkirk frowned and stepped out of the circle of children. "Is there something . . . " his voice was a nervous squeak, "something you have to tell me?" His eyelids were twitching.

"I think it would be better outside," Mike said.

"Don't worry about the children. I'll stay with them, Justin. Don't you worry about a thing." The tall woman spoke soothingly, as though to a child.

He looked gratefully at her. "Thank you, Lou-lou."

Mike spluttered and Joanna knew exactly what he was thinking. She had never met anyone who looked less like a Lou-lou herself.

They were outside the door before Justin Selkirk put his hand to his throat. "Tell me," he said theatrically, "please, don't spare me. What has happened to my father?"

Joanna's silence was cut short.

"He's dead?" he squeaked. "Oh, my God. My father. He's dead. Dead. Oh, do tell me. What happened?"

It was like a badly acted, badly scripted play. If this had been a screen audition Justin

Selkirk would have just flunked it.

"He's been shot," Mike said brutally. "We found him a short while ago."

Justin blinked and the awful charade began again. "Oh, my God." This time he clutched his forehead. "My own father. He shot himself?"

"We didn't say that." Mike was finding it hard to keep the dislike out of his voice.

Justin Selkirk looked at him, then at Joanna.

"He was found shot," she said quietly. "Obviously we can't tell you much more. We only discovered his body a couple of hours ago."

"Where?" Selkirk demanded.

"Gallows Wood."

Justin Selkirk blinked, then he gave a nervous laugh. "Gallows Wood?" he squeaked.

"Do you know it?" Joanna was suddenly curious.

"Yes, I mean, not really. I mean. I . . . "

The two detectives waited.

Selkirk swallowed. "We sometimes take the children beetle-spotting there. And once we saw the badgers too." He looked proud of himself. "I joined the badger protection society."

Mike gave a loud sigh.

"Mr Selkirk," Joanna said slowly. "We need someone to formally identify your father."

"Isn't it usually the next of kin?" he squeaked. "Have you asked my mother?"

Behind her Joanna heard Mike give an expression of disgust.

"Your father isn't a pretty sight," she said sharply. "He was shot in the head. We thought you might want to spare your mother."

Selkirk drew himself up to his full tiny height. "Of course," he said, now acting the gentleman. "Now?"

Joanna nodded. "We can take you to the mortuary in the police car," she said, "or if you prefer you can follow us in your own vehicle."

Selkirk nodded. "You'll have to wait a minute, I must tell Lou-lou."

They watched him through the wired glass speaking to the tall woman. Her face was tender with concern as she gave him a quick hug.

The children seemed to sense something was wrong and an unhappy wail started like a factory siren. Justin lowered himself to their height and spoke for a moment or two. It must have had some effect. The children's wailing faded away. One or two of them clapped their hands.

Justin stood up, gave a fond glance around the room, then approached the door. Joanna and Mike stood back.

"I'd rather use my car," he said. "My poor mother. I must go to her."

* * *

The morticians had laid Jonathan Selkirk out very carefully, a sheet hiding the missing portion of his face. To her surprise, when Joanna lifted the top sheet Justin Selkirk stared without emotion.

"That is my father," he said, before picking up his lines. "May God rest his soul."

It was Mike, standing directly behind Justin Selkirk, who noticed his fingers were weaving in and out of each other in frenzied activity.

Joanna only saw the beads of sweat on his brow and the frightened expression in his eyes when he finally stopped staring at his father.

"What happens now?"

"A lot," she said shortly. "We have to perform a post-mortem. Then there'll be an inquest, a police investigation." She watched him curiously. "Do you know anyone who would have wanted your father dead?"

Justin Selkirk gave a convulsive twitch. "Someone must have wanted to kill him," he squeaked. "Unless . . . a psychopath?" he finished lamely.

"Wandered into the hospital, picked on your father, got him into the car, bound his wrists, pushed him through the wood, persuaded him to kneel and shot him in the back of the head," Mike said brutally. "I don't think so, Mr Selkirk."

Joanna thought Justin would faint.

"My father's funeral?" he murmured.

"Not just yet," Joanna said. "We'll let you know when the body will be released for burial." She paused before adding, "Do you recognize his pyjamas?"

"Yes," he said.

"Your mother said she bought them new, a couple of days ago."

Selkirk looked perfectly comfortable. "My mother and I often go shopping together," he said. "We're very close." He hopped from one foot to the other. "Is that all? May I go now? I should visit my mother and my wife." He sounded like a polite little boy asking whether he was allowed to get down from the table.

"Yes, for now," Joanna said. "Of course we'll want to come round to your home and talk to you and your wife."

"Why?"

"Because," Joanna said patiently, "the more we know about your father's life the better the hope that we will find out who wanted him dead."

Selkirk moved closer. "It wasn't me," he said. "I absolutely adored my father. And he adored me," he finished defiantly.

Joanna didn't even need to look at Mike to know his expression.

Selkirk looked at one then the other and bolted.

The minute he had gone, Mike had a field day. He put his hand in a duck bill and strutted around the room with his bottom sticking out. "Oh, I often go shopping with my mummy," he mimicked in a falsetto, then, in disgust, "what a lady's blouse."

But Joanna held up a finger. "A married lady's blouse," she said, "who's fathered a child."

"Which only goes to show," Mike said, "how appearances can be deceptive."

"Yes, well," she said. "Whatever you may think, Mike, don't go jumping to conclusions."

Mike shrugged his shoulders. "My instincts tell me, Joanna," he said, grinning, "and I know how fond you are of instincts. I think he could have hated his father, who packed him off to school with no mercy. He could have hated him for years. But he couldn't have killed him himself. So he got someone to do it for him."

She looked at him shrewdly. "You think it was Selkirk?"

He nodded. "Could be. I've never seen such an awful pretence of grief," he said. "Pathetic little creep."

"Mike," Joanna said slowly, "you don't think Justin Selkirk had to act the part of grief because he'd felt nothing for his father — no love and therefore no grief — rather than that he hated him?"

"What's the difference?"

"A feeling of indifference rarely leads to murder, Mike, even if you get someone else to do it for you, but if he *hated* his father," she sighed, "it's possible."

Mike grunted and glanced down at the shrouded body. "I don't know about all that," he said. "Do you want me to stay for the PM, or do you want Levin all to yourself?"

"Along with half a dozen SOCOs and a couple of morticians?" She shook her head. "Go back to the station, Mike. Matthew will drop me off later. Tell someone to look into Mrs Selkirk's plans for the day. I suppose

I'd better speak to her this afternoon, and then we'd better get back to the hospital and check up on those statements, find out whether Selkirk did make a phone call." She sighed. "I have a feeling this is going to be a difficult nut to crack." Then she voiced her main fear, "If I'm allowed to keep it."

"Well," he said slowly. "I don't have much experience in this sort of field."

"What sort of field, Mike?" She paused, her eyes fixed on his face.

"Contract killing," he said and she nodded.

"Yes. Me neither. Ugly and professional. If I'm not very much mistaken, money has changed hands. Someone paid to have Selkirk executed."

★ ★ ★

Matthew was as usual in good spirits. He loved his work, loved the challenge of a corpse, loved the way it yielded up its secrets to his skilled fingers.

He was already dressed in his theatre green, gloves snapped on tight, scalpel blade fixed in its holder. He watched the mortician do the preliminary measurements before he examined the bullet hole.

"One hell of blast," he said. "Done a lot of

damage." He looked up at Joanna. "Found the bullet?"

She nodded. "Nine millimetre. Handgun." She grinned at him. "Bagged up and sent to forensics but one of the guys who knows a bit more about firearms has laid a bet it was a Beretta 92F. And there's something strange about the bullet."

"Very good." Matthew's eyes were bright with appreciation. "Would it be a hollow point?"

"Yes, that's it."

"So that explains the extensive destruction of the face. You took some specimens from the trees?"

"Quite a nature walk," she said.

"I was reading in an article the other day," he said, watching the mortician sawing through the skull with the electric drill, "written by some American guy with lots of experience in firearms, that the pattern of brain tissue can tell you exactly at what angle the person was to the assailant. Even how tall the assailant was."

Joanna thought she was going to be sick.

"Sorry." Matthew quickly apologized. "How's the arm?" he added cheerfully.

"Fine," she said. "Hardly hurts at all. In fact," she added, "if it wasn't for this," she rapped the plaster cast, "I'd have forgotten about it by now. But it has its uses. It rakes in plenty of sympathy and I get a free chauffeur."

"Doesn't life get a bit claustrophobic being cooped up in a car with Tarzan all day?"

"No," she said shortly. "Anyway, I told him you'd take me back to the station."

"Fine by me," he said. His face softened and he rested his arm on her shoulders. "I'm just glad it's all right and that you weren't worse hurt. It'll be perfect again soon. The wonders of modern medicine," he crowed.

"More like the wonders of ancient nature. Isn't it that that knits the bone?" She gestured to the corpse. "And now shall we return to the wonders of modern forensics?"

Matthew's attention was already back with his work. "I think," he said as he weighed the brain, "about nine tenths of it's missing. You'll find it in the forest . . . " He shot her a mischievous look, "or on the bottom of a policeman's shoe."

He worked quietly now, turning his attention back to the brain before giving a low whistle. "It never ceases to amaze me," he said, "what a lot of damage is done by one small bullet. Nine-millimetre sounds so tiny, doesn't it? But just blunt that point . . . "

She was silent, the overpowering smell of

disinfectant bringing on the familiar nausea.

An hour later Matthew summed up his findings. "Death was due to a single shot to the base of the brain," he said. "Our killer couldn't have chosen a better spot." His green eyes were luminous. "Death would have been instantaneous. Got the cerebellum and the medulla oblongata."

"Don't get technical, Matthew," she pleaded. "What are you saying in plain English?"

"As I suspected in Gallows Wood," he said. "An expert job, Joanna." He washed his hands and rasped them dry on the paper towel. "The man who shot Jonathan Selkirk knew his job as well as I know mine and you know yours. The injuries were sustained with the one small bullet." His face was sober.

"A Beretta?"

"I can't commit myself," he said. "All I can say is that it was a small handgun with a nine-millimetre bore. The injuries were incompatible with life. It was a neat, professional execution."

She blinked, watching him manoeuvre the elbow taps back.

"Even the rope used was good-quality yachting rope, non-slip and very strong. The killer came prepared. And the knots were vicious, cut right into the flesh — a slip knot looped around, pulled tight and fastened. He wouldn't have got out of those in a month of Sundays."

He turned and grinned. "Oh, and by the way," he said. "Just as an added twist, Selkirk had had an MI."

She looked enquiringly at him. "MI?" she said. "Plain English, *please*."

"Myocardial infarct," he said cheerily. "Heart attack. Quite a big one too, clot the size of a mushroom lodged in one of the coronary arteries. He wasn't going to make it anyway."

Matthew started filling out the PM form. "Whoever it was who wanted him out of the way could have saved themselves a lot of money."

"Matthew, we don't *know* that it was a professional job yet. We — "

"Jo, I know I'm just a humble thick pathologist, and you're the clever police. I carve the corpse, tell you what they've done. You find out who and why and make a nuisance of yourselves to the CPS. But in my humble opinion, the villain who abducted Jonathan Selkirk from his — much needed — hospital bed only to drive him to Gallows Wood and pop a bullet in the back of his neck was paid to do it. This is as professional as I've seen in my entire career. The question you're going to have to address, my darling, as you know full well, is who picked up the bill? And who do you know with no morals but expertise. How many professional killers do you know, Joanna?"

She looked at him. "None."

6

Colclough's face sagged like a bloodhound's as Joanna related the findings of the post-mortem. "I don't like it, Piercy," he said. "This is a peaceful town. I've lived here all my life. I was born here. My mother came from Leek." He got out of his chair and wandered across to the window. Unlike the view from her office, his stretched right across the town, taking in the spire of the church, the war monument, the cobbled market square. He watched umbrellas scurrying along the High Street, people sheltering in doorways.

"This is a traditional town," he said. "People are brought up here, live here, die here." He turned around and she saw traces of an idealistic young copper, almost obliterated now by time. "This is a safe place. A little old-fashioned and traditional. When you arrest someone here you know their stock." He gave Joanna the ghost of a smile. "You're a newcomer here, Piercy."

"Six years, sir."

He nodded. "A newcomer, so let me tell you, contract killing is a shocking thing. An evil mind hiring an evil hand. Jonathan

Selkirk was an unpleasant man, but this
. . . to be dragged from a hospital bed and
shot." A look of pain shadowed his face.

"Did you know him well, sir?" she asked
curiously.

"Not as well as I do his wife." Colclough
flopped down in his seat. "He was an
outsider. She met him at university."

Joanna was mildly surprised. "She was at
university too?"

"She was cleverer than he, got an honours
degree but she never practised. As soon as
they were married she gave up and stayed
at home. A waste, Piercy, of a very good
brain. It was a shame their son took after
neither of them."

"Why did she give up?"

Colclough shrugged. "Who knows? Some
men prefer their wives to stay at home.
It seems Jonathan Selkirk was one of
them. After all, they weren't short of
money. Jonathan's practice was flourishing."
Colclough hesitated. "Between you and me,
Piercy, I rather think he liked the control.
A wife who works . . . " His bulldog chins
wobbled disapprovingly, as he picked up his
pen. "Now then, about this case. It's out of
our league, you know."

She'd been afraid he would do this — take
the case away from her. "But, sir . . . "

"Out of our league," he repeated. "Out of your league." He thought for a minute, stroked his chins. "And out of mine. Contract killings affect internal security, Piercy. I think I'd better inform the Regional Crime Squad. I'll make a couple of phone calls. Leave it with me." He narrowed his eyes. "What are you up to now?"

"I'm going to interview Selkirk's widow," she said.

"OK," he said. "For now you're in charge."

And she could guess the rest.

★ ★ ★

There was no sign of mourning outside the Georgian red brick house. As the car drew up both she and Mike noticed lights blazing out into the dull September afternoon.

"Looks more like Christmas," Mike observed.

"Perhaps they've cause to celebrate."

"You'd think they'd draw the curtains at least, as a mark of respect. She's just lost her husband."

"I don't think they did respect him," she said quietly and waited while he parked the car neatly next to a maroon Jaguar. "They do know he's been found?"

111

"Oh yes," Mike said. "A couple of uniformed guys called round earlier."

They walked round the Jaguar, peering in through the windows. All was neat and in order. A well-kept car with this year's registration number.

They approached the house and immediately there was another surprise. A child's peal of laughter could be heard ringing out from the garden.

"It's a different house," Joanna said. "I feel as though we've come to the wrong place. It's alive."

They were drawn towards the laughter. Instead of knocking on the front door they skirted the house to the broad green lawn speckled with early fallen leaves. The Shirley Temple lookalike and Jonathan Selkirk's widow were raking them up. Joanna and Mike watched them for a while, scraping the lawn and forming tiny heaps of damp leaves. Especially the child. She was a laughing, chattering little thing, a pretty, picture-book toddler in scarlet anorak and elf-green trousers running around in tiny red wellies and tossing her thick mop of golden curls. And as she laughed she held up her hands to try to steal the leaves from the wind's gusts. Then Sheila Selkirk stopped and leaned against her rake, the heap of leaves quickly dispersing as the wind found them again. She was watching the child with such a look of absorbed happiness that Joanna was reminded of classical paintings of Madonna with Adored Child. This scene was so far removed from the ugly site of execution at Gallows Wood that she was reluctant to remind Sheila Selkirk of her husband's murder and instead stood stock still. She glanced at Mike and knew he too was lured by this captivating picture.

At length she cleared her throat. "Mrs Selkirk."

Sheila Selkirk froze. The spell was broken. The child stopped laughing and ran to her grandmother, flung her arms around her legs. Her face was sharp and frightened. Selkirk's widow stood, paralyzed.

"Inspector Piercy," she said. "I knew you'd come." Her voice was strained and held a faint tinge of guilt. For what? For enjoying herself? Or was there some other reason?

Sheila looked from one to the other and must have read some of their disapproval. "Whatever else I may be, Inspector," she said defensively, "I am no hypocrite. I have here," her hand rested on the child's bouncing curls, "my consolation."

Her lips worked nervously. "There is no use my sitting and mourning him, pretending.

Jonathan's dead. In my heart of hearts, from the moment he went missing from the hospital I knew he was." She gave a tight smile. "I was just wrong in some of the details. I imagined . . . " She stopped and looked past them at two gnarled trees at the corner of the lawn. "I somehow imagined that pressure of work and financial problems combined with a certain pessimism in his character had driven him to take his own life." She stopped. "I was wrong. Someone came round from your station earlier. They've already given me most the details." A shadow crossed her face. "I know he was shot. And Justin came round straight from the morgue." She swallowed. "I think I know most of the facts." She stared boldly at them, challenging them.

Their attention was diverted by the child who was holding up her arms and tugging impatiently at her grandmother's coat. Sheila Selkirk swept her up and hugged her tight. "My little darling," she cooed. She looked up. "Teresa came round this morning with little Lucy, to cheer me up. Wasn't that kind?"

She set the child down on the path and turned to face the inviting yellow lights of the house. "Teresa's inside now, talking to Tony. Please, do come in, both of you. I'm ready for a cup of tea anyway . . . And you, my little princess," she said to the child, "could do with some orange juice."

The child chuckled and skipped along the path, calling after her, "Grandma . . . Grandma . . . "

Mike gave Joanna a swift, puzzled glance as they entered the house through the back door and she knew what he was thinking. The ugly murder of Jonathan Selkirk seemed not to have touched his family. Could someone really be so unlovable? Could a family be so unfeeling? This was wrong. It was indecent. They should be showing some appearance of grief, however superficial.

Even so, she touched Mike's shoulder. "Don't judge her too harshly," she whispered. "Perhaps she's just a stoic."

Mike shrugged. "I don't know what she bloody well is," he said, "but I'd like to think my wife would have a bit more feeling if my brains had been splattered all over a local wood."

Inside the kitchen Sheila was peeling off Lucy's wellies. She set them side by side near the Aga before putting pink slippers on the small feet. "Now then, my little darling," she said. "Let's go and find Mummy and Grandpa Tony." The child disappeared through the door and the adults followed.

115

The sitting room had been transformed. The room was warm, bright and cosy. Photographs now covered the surface of the piano. A quick glance and Joanna saw baby photographs, wedding photographs, couples, old people. She saw Justin Selkirk with his arm round a black-haired young woman and plenty of little Lucy. It was as though Sheila Selkirk had suddenly come alive and found depth and background, family and friends. She peered closer but failed to find even one of Jonathan Selkirk with his humourless face and toothbrush moustache.

There were two people in the room, sitting either side of a bright gas fire. Their conversation stopped as the police walked in. One was a middle-aged man with thick white hair. The other was the pale-faced woman with black hair from the photograph. She gave them a sharp, hostile glance as they entered, then she leaned forward and stubbed out a cigarette in a saucer.

"I shall have to buy some ashtrays," Sheila Selkirk said happily before sitting down on the sofa. "These are the police, my dears, investigating what happened to poor old Jonathan."

"Poor old Jonathan." It sounded as though he had had a minor prang in his car.

"This is my daughter-in-law, Teresa," she

said, and this is my old friend Tony Pritchard. And you already know Lucy."

The child scrambled on to her mother's lap and burrowed her head into her breast.

The black-haired woman was heavily pregnant. Her dark eyes were fixed on Sheila Selkirk. "Mother?" she said anxiously.

The older woman was quick to reassure her. "It's all right, Teresa, my dear," she said.

Joanna felt an outsider, looking in — not on grief but on a family celebration.

"I'm sorry to intrude," she said to the seated pair. "But I do need to speak to Mrs Selkirk alone."

The man stood up, moved swiftly across the room and put a protective arm around Sheila Selkirk's shoulders. "Darling," he said, "do you want me to stay?"

She laughed. "No, Grandpa Tony." The name seemed a private joke between them. "Of course not." She turned and gave him an affectionate glance. "I'm a big girly now."

The man looked dubious. "Anything you want to say to Sheila," he said to the two police officers, "can be said in front of me."

"Oh, no, it bloody well can't!" Mike said. "Look, Mr . . . "

"Pritchard," the man said tightly. "Sheila

117

did tell you my name."

"Jonathan Selkirk was murdered two nights ago," Mike said. "He was dragged from his hospital bed, his hands were tied behind his back and" — he glanced at the child still watching her mother — "well, I think you know the rest." And he jabbed two fingers into the back of his neck as if to illustrate. "Bang. Finito."

Everyone in the room winced.

"Whether you like it or not," he continued, "it's our job to find out who did it . . . or, more to the point, who picked up the tab. None of you lot seems to care who it was. We get here today and find you playing Happy Families . . . Grandpa Tony," he finished in disgust.

Sheila Selkirk was pale. "What do you mean? Picked up the tab?"

"It's possible," Mike said slowly, looking at each of them in turn, "that someone paid to have Jonathan Selkirk murdered. His death shows signs of a professional job. Now, what's going on?"

The two women looked stunned. Sheila Selkirk opened her mouth but said nothing. The child looked up from playing with her mother's long string of beads, her eyes large and shrewd.

It was left to Anthony Pritchard to take a

step forward and he too was pale. He cleared his throat noisily.

"You didn't know Jonathan Selkirk," he said in a low, controlled voice. "He was a bastard. A bastard of the first order. Ask anyone who knew him. In his professional life as well as in his home he was an utter bastard. He spread misery. The world," he said decisively, "is a better place without him. Ask anyone."

"We will," Joanna said crisply. "We will."

She looked around the room. The venom in everyone's faces seemed to taint the air.

"Are you trying to tell us it was you who paid to have him shot?" Joanna asked smoothly, staring at the eagle face in front of her. She smiled encouragingly at him. "Or, failing that, that you shot him yourself, Mr Pritchard?"

"Absolutely not," he said vehemently, "Absolutely not. So you needn't think you can force some sort of confession out of me. But I can tell you, Inspector, you won't have to look very far at all to find many people who would have given money to have Selkirk out of the way." He paused for breath.

"Anyone in particular, Mr Pritchard?"

"Two or three. Try speaking to Wilde to start with."

Joanna drew out her notebook.

Sheila Selkirk shot Pritchard a swift, warning look.

He ignored it. "Rufus Wilde, Solicitor," he said. "Partners in crime. You can start by finding out what they were up to."

"Thank you for your help."

Pritchard made a mock bow.

Joanna watched the pregnant woman cuddling the child, then she focused her attention back on the widow. "We're still waiting to interview you alone," she said.

Sheila Selkirk's fine, dark eyes mocked Joanna. "Do I have any choice about this, Inspector?"

Joanna fixed her face into a smile. "Yes," she said. "Of course you do. You have the choice of talking to us here or at the station. I really don't mind where but we will speak to you, Mrs Selkirk, or charge you with obstruction."

Sheila Selkirk glared at Joanna for a while then bowed her head. "There's no need for that," she said quietly and with dignity before turning to the white-haired man. "Anthony, darling, put the kettle on."

Tony Pritchard disappeared, muttering.

Selkirk's widow crossed the room, bent and kissed her daughter-in-law on the cheek. "Thank you so much for coming, my dear, and for bringing this little ray of sunshine with you." She tweaked the child's cheek. "And of course I'll be delighted to look after her when you go into hospital."

Teresa Selkirk smiled vague thanks and set the child on the floor, her pregnancy more obviously cumbersome when she stood up. A thought flashed through Joanna's mind. How ugly and ungainly pregnancy was. Never for her. Never for her, whatever Matthew thought.

Sheila Selkirk seemed to think her daughter-in-law needed more reassurance. "You're not to worry. Everything is going to be quite all right." She hugged her.

Teresa gave a faint smile. The child was standing still, watching them both with round, noticing eyes. Sheila Selkirk bent and kissed her too. "Goodbye, my darling," she said. "I'll see you both tomorrow."

Lucy slipped her hand in her mother's and then they were gone, leaving Mike, Joanna and Sheila Selkirk sitting alone.

Sheila faced them brightly. "As I said, Inspector, I will not be a hypocrite. My life with Jonathan was not happy." She paused. "It was — a cross I had to bear."

Mike's face was puce.

Sheila sank back down on the sofa, frowning. "Is it true," she asked, "that his hands were tied behind his back?" Without waiting for an answer she muttered, "They didn't tell me that . . . They didn't tell me that."

"So bloody tight, Mrs Selkirk, the rope bit his flesh."

Joanna gave Mike an angry glance. Whatever his private thoughts, there was no need for this.

"Mrs Selkirk," she began. "Your husband was killed, murdered. There is no doubt about that." She stopped. "We think he was almost certainly murdered by a professional. We believe someone was paid to shoot him."

Sheila Selkirk looked startled. "I see." She sat waiting, her hands folded on her lap, eyes fixed on Joanna's face.

"Mrs Selkirk." Joanna moved along the sofa, a little closer. "Who would have wanted your husband dead?" She paused to let her words take effect. "Or let's put it another way. Who would have paid money to have your husband killed?"

For a long time Sheila Selkirk was silent, biting her lips. Neither Joanna nor Mike could be sure whether the pause was for effect or because she really was pondering the point.

Eventually she spoke, in a calm, controlled voice. "Lots of people had reason to dislike

Jonathan. He was that sort of person, a rough-edged man. People didn't like him. He rubbed them up the wrong way. You see, Inspector . . . "

Joanna reflected that she being was addressed rather than Mike because as a woman she might show more sympathy. If that was what Sheila Selkirk believed, she was wrong.

"Jonathan liked to control people. He was a bully." She stopped and thought for a minute. "He was abrasive, opinionated. He always had to be right. But people aren't killed for that, are they?" There was something uneasy about her look now. Difficult to read. "Maybe . . . maybe someone to do with his work? He met some very unpleasant types, you know."

"Yes, Mrs Selkirk?"

"I don't know." She looked confused. "I don't know. He didn't discuss his work with me, although . . . " Her voice faltered, her confidence ebbing like the tide.

"Although he might have done?"

Sheila Selkirk grimaced.

"After all, you have a law degree too, don't you?"

Joanna must have touched a raw nerve.

"What's that got to do with you?" the woman snapped. "It's irrelevant. Anyway, I think we can discount the local villains, can't we?" She looked at Mike this time. "They wouldn't have needed to pay someone else, would they?" she asked with a touch of black humour. "I mean, they could have done it themselves. He did defend murderers."

"Please think," Joanna said, struck with an idea of her own. "Was your husband ever involved in defending someone who used firearms?"

She thought for a moment. "I seem to remember reading something and asking him whether he was involved in the defence. I'm sorry," she said. "I can't remember the man's name."

Mike looked interested. "How long ago?"

"Eight, ten years ago. I can't remember. The man was put away for life."

Both Mike and Joanna were thinking exactly the same thought. Put away — for eight to ten years.

"And Wilde?"

She rolled her eyes. "Sometimes, Inspector, solicitors are worse crooks than the villains they're defending."

Joanna nodded. "Do you know anyone who has a handgun?"

"No."

"Do you have a handgun?"

She shook her head. "It was that damned

letter!" she said, in the first display of emotion. "If it hadn't been for that damned letter nothing would have happened."

"Ah yes," Joanna said. "Back to the letter."

Sheila Selkirk stared. "Are you trying to tell me you think that letter was genuine?" She paused. "That it's connected with his death?"

"It might be," Joanna said cautiously. "It would be rather a coincidence otherwise, wouldn't it?"

Sheila Selkirk blinked rapidly. "I see what you mean." She was visibly shaken. "Oh," she said. "How horrible."

"Isn't it?"

"So when he was upset that morning . . . ?"

"It would seem that your husband had an inkling of what was in store. Please think, Mrs Selkirk. Did he say who he thought had sent it?"

She looked away. "No," she said.

"You're sure?" Mike was staring at her.

She nodded. "Yes," she said. "He didn't know who had sent it."

"He didn't even have an idea?"

"I said not." She was beginning to look annoyed.

"And you said that he had never received anything like that before?"

"That's what I said." And she fixed her

eyes on Joanna's face as though pleading to be believed.

★ ★ ★

Mike looked at her in the car. "What a household," he said. "That poor beggar."

"Selkirk was no beggar," Joanna said. "And he was not poor. But I agree. It would be nice to think someone would mourn you."

He grinned at her. "How's the arm?"

She picked it up experimentally. "A bit sore," she said. "But nothing too bad."

"That plaster looks like a deadly weapon, Jo."

She nodded. "So mind your Ps and Qs, Sergeant."

"So where now?"

"I think back to the hospital," she said. "I want to talk to the other nurses on duty on Monday night. If he made a phone call I want to know who to." She gave a swift glance at the radio telephone. "I suppose we'd better call in first."

★ ★ ★

But Colclough had other ideas.

"I want you in here within half an hour,

126

Piercy." His determination was unmistakable.

She rolled her eyes at Mike. "Typical," she raged. "I'm just opening enquiries. I don't want to lose this case, Mike."

"You want a bit of advice, Inspector?"

She nodded.

"You've got no bloody option," he said grimly.

★ ★ ★

Colclough's face was grim. "I don't expect you to like this," he warned, "but the Regional Crime Squad will be taking over the case from tomorrow morning."

She found it hard to keep her temper.

He read the disappointment as well as the anger in her face. "I'm sorry, Piercy," he said, "but this isn't a job for us local bobbies. It might be part of something quite big. A racket. The person who shot Selkirk might even be an international killer. We can't take the risk."

"Of messing it up?"

"Don't be awkward, Piercy. This is a policy decision made above your head."

She sat down heavily. Her arm ached. "But, sir," she pleaded. "This is a local case. He was a local man. Already I'm beginning to make inroads. My investigations are unearthing things, possible motives. The family, sir . . . "

"Good God, Piercy," Colclough exclaimed. "I thought you understood. This isn't some poxy little family squabble. I've read the pathologist's report — twice. This was almost certainly an organized professional contract killing."

"Sir . . . That may be. But it was still someone local, with a personal motive, who forked out the cash. There's more to this than just a bullet in the brain. Someone wanted him dead and very badly. The reasons, sir, are not international. They are local."

"We have to get the Regional Crime Squad. They'll be here in the morning. Joanna, hasn't it occurred to you? We want someone from outside the area — a stranger. We don't want there to be a possibility of retaliation."

7

Mike watched her walk back into the office.

"Bad news?"

"The worst." She made a face. "We've lost the case. He's handing over to the Regional Crime Squad." She spat the words out.

He said nothing.

"Honestly, Mike. All this crap about internal security. Given time, we'd easily have cracked it."

"Would we?"

She sat down in the chair opposite him. "Well, we might have had trouble actually finding the gunman," she conceded, "but we'd have made good inroads." Her frustration surfaced again. "Damn! Now I've got to hand over all our notes, all the interviews. The bloody lot." She scowled. "All that hard work. It simply isn't fair."

Mike sat back in his chair. "So what now?"

She looked at his glum face and knew he felt it every bit as badly as she did.

"We could just visit the hospital," she suggested. "Talk to the other night nurses again. Just in case there's something we've missed."

"And then what?"

"Then I'm going to drown my sorrows with Matthew," she said. "He says he's bought me a present, and I could do with something to cheer me up. Now, let's get back to the hospital."

★ ★ ★

They were in luck. Two of the three nurses were on duty in the coronary ward. Only Yolande Prince was missing.

The nursing officer looked at them. "Not surprisingly the poor girl has phoned in sick. Such a shock," she said disapprovingly. "I told her mother she mustn't rush back. She needs time."

Then she stared at Joanna. "Don't go giving the poor child hassle, unless you absolutely have to. She's very vulnerable . . . very upset. She had a bad experience last year — upset her terribly. I had great trouble persuading her to continue working here at all. And now this." She shook her head. "The poor girl seems dogged by ill luck. Such a shame . . . such a shame. An excellent nurse."

"We'll leave her alone for a few days,"

Joanna said. "I really wanted to talk to the other two nurses today."

"That's all right, then. They aren't quite so sensitive as Yolande. Of course, she was in charge of the ward. So ultimately the blame does, I'm afraid, rest on her shoulders."

For all her sympathy, Joanna thought, she was as detached as a judge passing sentence. The nursing officer stood up. "Use my office. I'll send for Nurse Richards and Mr O'Sullivan." She managed to inject a large amount of disapproval into the latter name and Joanna gave Mike a swift, curious glance.

Gaynor Richards was short and tubby, almost as wide as she was tall. The buttons of her nurse's uniform gaped and strained over her plump body as she rushed in, breathless and anxious to please.

After the introductions Joanna opened the questioning. "Do you remember Mr Selkirk being admitted?"

She nodded. "The day staff actually admitted him," she said. "He came in in the middle of the morning. By the time we came on duty he'd calmed down a bit." She looked from one to the other. "He wasn't very well. Muttered a lot. Seemed very worried." The nurse kept smiling at both of them for no

131

apparent reason. It was beginning to irritate Joanna.

"Did you talk to him?"

"Yes, I just told him everything would be all right," she said happily. "A couple of nights in here, I told him, and you'll be right as rain. Though," she added, "he was very unwell."

"Well," Joanna smiled encouragingly, "I expect that cheered him up."

"I think it did," she said, leaning forward. A button popped open and she grabbed the two edges of the dress and tugged them together desperately. "They like to be cheered up."

"Did he have any visitors?"

"Oh no!" She looked horrified. "He was far too ill to be having people traipsing through wanting to see him. He had to be kept quiet." She blinked at them. "Wives only. His wife was there for some of the evening." She hesitated, looked at Joanna then Mike and shut her mouth.

"They seemed good friends?" Joanna asked casually.

Gaynor Richards blinked. "Being ill's such a strain," she said. "On the relatives as well as the patient. It's very difficult." She looked uneasy and they guessed that Sheila Selkirk and her husband had been arguing.

132

"You spoke to Mrs Selkirk?"

"I made her a cup of tea." She looked pleased with herself.

"Did she say anything to you?"

"She wanted to know about his condition."

"What did you tell her?"

Gaynor Richards blinked and forgot to smile. "We don't give away confidential details about our patients," she said blandly. "The doctors speak to relatives."

"She spoke to the doctor?"

The nurse shook her head. "He wasn't around. I told her she could talk to him the next day, but she said it didn't matter." She screwed up her face. "I don't think she understood how ill he was."

Joanna sighed. "Perhaps you reassured her a bit too well."

Gaynor Richards looked happy and unconcerned.

"You spoke to Mr Selkirk?"

"I took him a drink at nine," the nurse said, "just after his wife left. Then he asked if he could use the phone."

"And?"

"I got it for him," she said. "But he didn't have change. The hospital telephone is one of those pay phones that you can't reverse charges on. No money and he wouldn't be able to make any calls." She thought for a moment. "His wife had taken his clothes, you see. She probably forgot to leave him any money." Again she looked uncomfortable and they could picture Selkirk ranting about being left penniless.

"So did he make a call or not?"

"I don't know," Gaynor said, unconscious of the two police officers' frustration. "I got called to the far end of the ward. But I didn't take the phone from him. I just left it there." She thought for a moment, then said brightly, "He might have made a call, mightn't he?"

"So you don't know whether he made a call at all, let alone who to?" Mike grunted.

The nurse shook her head. "Not really. Sorry."

"Did he say anything else to you?"

Again she thought for a moment, then shook her head. "No," she said, "I don't think so." She leaned forward to share her confidence. "I think he just wanted to be quiet — to be left alone."

"And the last time you saw him?"

"About half past ten," Gaynor said. "You see, I thought that if he was going to be making a phone call — she gave another one of her irritating, ingratiating smiles and tweaked her buttons together — "I thought — with him being a solicitor and all that — I thought he'd want a bit of privacy. So I shut the door." She gave each of them a triumphant smile. "I didn't see him after that. And that was hours before he went."

Joanna gave Mike a swift glance before looking back at the self-satisfied face of the nurse. "What time did he go?" she asked casually.

Gaynor almost jumped out of her chair. "I don't know," she said. "I really don't. I just heard . . . "

"What did you hear?" Mike's voice was velvet-soft.

She stared at him "They said about one."

"Who said?"

"Staff Nurse."

"Yolande Prince?"

Gaynor nodded. And she pressed her lips together while her eyes were wide and staring.

They let her go out of pity.

As the door closed behind her Mike groaned. "Well, she was a fat lot of use," he said.

Joanna was staring at the closed door. "Is she really as dull as she seems?" she asked thoughtfully. "All this cheering people up . . . didn't know whether he'd used the phone or not . . . told him he'd be all right when the man knew he'd had a heart attack . . . " She looked at Mike. "And challenging her how she knew the time Selkirk was abducted. That sent her into a panic, didn't it?" She stopped. "The question is does she ring true? Is she stupid or is she clever?"

"Stupid," Mike said firmly. "Believe me. That girl hasn't any sense in her head."

"We'll see," Joanna uncrossed her legs. "Mike," she said softly, her face puckered in a deep frown. "There's something we haven't really considered."

He waited, catching the scent of newly washed hair. That must be for Levin, he thought.

"How did our killer know where to find Selkirk?" she said. "He was only admitted that day. But we have no stories of someone looking into all the rooms. No one." She stopped for the full implication of her words to sink in. "Our killer knew not only that Selkirk was in hospital but how to get in and which room he was in."

Mike nodded slowly.

"So our killer was in contact with his employer that day."

"Yes."

She sat back. "Who knew Selkirk was in hospital?"

"His wife and almost certainly his partner in crime, Wilde. He would have to know," He paused. "But Sheila wasn't going to tell him," he said. "Bit of trouble there if I'm not mistaken."

"Maybe that's why he was so desperate to use the phone."

"In the day, maybe," Mike said thoughtfully. "But our friend Gaynor was talking about the evening, just after his wife had gone home." He met her eyes. "Checking up on her?"

"Possibly," she said. "And maybe her taking away his clothes and money was a clever idea so he wouldn't be able to use the phone."

"We've forgotten someone else who knew Selkirk was in hospital," he said. "Grandpa Tony."

Joanna nodded.

"Now let's meet nurse number three."

Ian O'Sullivan proved to be a thin-faced man in his mid twenties, pale skinned with mischievous blue eyes.

"Hello there," he said when Joanna introduced herself and Mike. "I wondered when you'd be getting around to me."

Joanna raised her eyebrows. "Well, we're here now and want to know anything you can tell us about Mr Selkirk."

"I was the one who helped him settle in,"

O'Sullivan said proudly. "So I was probably the one who spoke the most to him. That wife of his," he continued, "wasn't she just the frosty one."

"Was she?" Mike asked innocently.

"Glad she was that he was sufferin'. I could see it in her eyes. Takin' pleasure in it," he added maliciously.

"But she left around," Joanna glanced down at her notes, "nine?"

"He watched her go." O'Sullivan was enjoying telling his tale. "Watched her close the door behind her. And then he asked Fatty Richards if he could use the phone." O'Sullivan stopped and swallowed. "Bloody desperate he was to get at that phone."

"But Nurse Richards told us he had no money to use it."

O'Sullivan looked pleased with himself. "I lent him some," he said. "I could tell he wasn't short of a bob or two. I knew I'd get it back, with interest. I lent him five twenty-pence pieces. Although I don't suppose I'll get it back at all now."

Mike's breath was quickening. "Who did he call?"

The nurse leaned back and folded his arms. "Now how should I know?" Then he winked at Joanna. "To be sure, I didn't listen all the way through. All I heard was a couple of words. He said something was wild." He grinned. "You know — wild, man?"

Joanna frowned. "Wild?"

"I would have heard more," he said, "if that bloody bitch of a staff nurse hadn't got me cleaning up some shit." He gave Joanna a sly look. "And there's another mystery that's never been cleared up." He stopped and leered at Joanna. "I'll bet she didn't tell you anything about that poor bastard who fell out of the window. Last year."

"She did mention that she'd had some trouble last year — "

"It was her was on duty that night." O'Sullivan said with feeling.

Joanna drummed her fingers impatiently on the desk. "I don't really think this is relevant," she said sharply.

"Oh, don't you?" O'Sullivan's eyes were cruel. "I have an idea you're probably wrong there. And the enquiry don't know the half of it. But they needn't think I'll be the one to tell them." His eyes met Joanna's and he gave a quick wink. "She must have moved the chair, you know."

"Sorry? Which chair?" Joanna asked, confused now.

"Frost's." O'Sullivan said disdainfully. "Michael Frost's."

And for some reason they both listened.

"The window that that bloody madman Frost fell out of was more than six feet from the floor," he said. "How did he get up there? Especially on the medication he was on. He would have been like a bloody zombie. He couldn't have climbed six inches from the floor, let alone six feet. And I'm telling you this, there was no chair there — not by the window he was supposed to have jumped from. So how the hell did he get up there? Enquiries," he finished disgustedly. "Askin' all the wrong questions, they are."

Joanna gave in. After a quick gesture at Mike she asked, "Who exactly is Frost?"

"Was." O'Sullivan was excited now. "Or, to put it another bloody way, He Is No Longer With Us. He's dead. She sat on the bed for a bloody hour, leavin' me to do all the damned work. And that was that."

They stared at him and he gave a smirk. "The cow didn't tell you, did she?"

They shook their heads.

"Staff Nurse Prince," he said rudely. "No. This Selkirk business is not the first bit of *trouble* she's had. It was about a year or so ago she was on night duty. Michael Frost was a patient." He grinned. "Sorry, a depressed patient. She thought she could play the part of God and the Virgin Mary rolled into one. Only something went wrong. He dived out of the window. Dead." His blue eyes met Joanna's confidently. "Bit of a coincidence, don't you think? Two patients, two violent deaths, one nurse."

"O'Sullivan," Joanna said. "We aren't here to discuss what happened to Michael Frost. We're investigating the abduction and murder of Jonathan Selkirk."

"Maybe they're connected," the Irishman said, tapping the side of his nose in an age-old gesture. "And I don't suppose that bitch of a Staff Nurse told you the half of it, did she?"

Mike stood up.

"The family sent letters to the hospital. Nasty letters. You see, Frost had a sister. And she was very upset about it. Now, if you've got any sense," he said, "you'll be looking into all that." He stood up and leaned towards her. His thin face was deeply scored with spite.

"The trouble with witnesses like that," Joanna said when O'Sullivan had finally gone, "is that you never know how much is truth, how much is spite and how much pure bloody fiction."

Mike agreed. "Are you going to look into this Michael Frost business?"

Joanna thought for a moment. "Well," she said finally. "If I'm to be taken off

141

Jonathan Selkirk's little hole in the head I suppose I might as well do a little research of my own into this 'unfortunate happening at the hospital'." She looked at him. "But I don't honestly think the two incidents are connected. I'm sure it's coincidence that Yolande Prince was on duty during them both." She stopped. "I have no suspicions of her at all. And the moment the RCS have finished with their part of the case I'm going to find out who footed the bill for Selkirk's picnic in Gallows Wood."

Mike's eyes warmed as he watched her. "Glad to see you're not going to give up, Jo," he said.

She frowned. "Definitely not. But O'Sullivan did say one thing that interested me," she said. "He mentioned the name Wilde. The name of Selkirk's partner."

"Perhaps we'd better pay him a visit."

"Not now." She glanced at her watch. "Mike, drop me off at the cottage, will you? I'm going to be late."

★ ★ ★

She was late. The smell of scorched food greeted her as she opened the front door.

She found Matthew in the kitchen. "Sorry," she said. "I'm so sorry."

"You might have rung, Joanna," he said peevishly and she knew he was angry.

"I really am sorry." She sighed. "I've actually had a pig of a day." She opened the oven door and looked at the dried-up lasagne. "Mmmm," she said.

"It was quite nice an hour ago, Joanna," he said severely.

She put her good arm around his neck. "We could get a take-away," she suggested.

"It isn't so bad that we have to abandon it." He was laughing now.

It was one of the many things she loved about Matthew. He was never in poor humour for long. He grinned.

"I've been listening to the news," he said. "And I didn't hear about any arrest yet."

He spooned some of the lasagne on to plates and carried them through with a large bowl of salad as she told him her news.

"So the Regional Crime Squad are poised to swoop," she concluded gloomily. "One of the most intriguing cases ever to hit the Moorlands and the bloody RCS have to dip their paws in."

He commiserated with her while they ate and when they had finished he cleared away and he filled their glasses. Then he handed her a square box, prettily wrapped in white paper with shiny red love hearts and a huge red bow.

"For you," he said. "To cheer you up."

"I can't open it, Matthew," she said, stupidly excited like a child on Christmas morning. "Not with this thing on my arm."

"Let me." He ripped off the paper and she saw the box.

Matthew's face was tense. "I knew as soon as you were out of plaster you'd be back on your bike. I just want you to be safe, Joanna, and your old one was damaged in the accident. If you hadn't been wearing it . . ."

"All right, all right," she said hastily. "Don't go into all the gory details. I know. I had a close shave. I'll be more careful in future."

"No, you won't." Matthew said soberly. "I've seen the way you tear around on your bike." There was a touch of grim humour in his eyes. "It's the speed you enjoy — and the danger. Your accident was inevitable. It was simply a matter of when, and how badly you'd be hurt."

"Matthew."

He put his arm around her and drew her close to him.

"There's no point telling daredevils like you to be careful." He tapped the shell of the helmet. "All I can do is buy you safety gear."

She was silent.

There was so much that he was avoiding saying, but it chastened her all the same. He wasn't reminding her that he had left a wife, a home, a child for her and that in return she had given him nothing. She wasn't even careful of her own safety, and her job invariably won priorities. But he had said nothing. It was only on occasions like this that she was reminded of it all. And the knowledge dragged guilt in its wake, like a heavy ball and chain. With Matthew came responsibilities and commitment. It could never be a free, pure love because its price had been too high. A sudden flash came to her, remembered from her childhood, of an elderly, maiden aunt pointing out a divorced man walking with his new wife, arm in arm, staring into each other's eyes, their steps jaunty. "Happiness can never be bought with misery," her aunt had said grimly. "Think of the poor wife." Joanna's round, child's eyes had absorbed the couple's apparent contentment and she had doubted what she had seen. When she recalled the scene later on that night she seemed to remember the couple's faces were sad and their steps slow. Now she looked at Matthew with that exact trace of sadness and shivered.

She felt agitated and cornered. "Matthew," she said softly.

He was watching her with that steady, quizzical look that made his face appear thin. He was waiting for her to give him her time, her affection, her commitment.

"Matthew," she said again, awkwardly.

He stroked her hair. "I couldn't bear to lose you," he said, and then in an abrupt change of subject he picked up the helmet. "Come here. Let's try it for size."

She put it on her head and Matthew tightened the strap beneath her chin. He kissed her. "It'll give me some peace of mind," he said, "next time I hear you've surfaced in casualty."

She took it off and laid it back in its box with a sigh. "How long will it be," she said, "before I'm back on my bike?"

"Be patient," he urged. "Not long." He watched her for a moment and she sensed his unease. "You haven't forgotten about tomorrow night, have you?"

She shook her head.

"You don't mind, do you?"

She minded. She minded very much and he knew it. But he would always ask, maybe in the hope that one day her 'no' would be the truth. "No," she said.

★ ★ ★

They sat like a courting couple, talking and playing Mozart, punctuating the evening with soft, slow kisses that never quite boiled but simmered for hours, until the sound of the telephone shrilled into their peace and Colclough's weary voice told her someone called Pugh would be occupying her office from ten a.m. in the morning. Would she be good enough to clear the desk? Early.

8

Her temper was already roused by the time Mike picked her up in the morning.

"Damn this bloody plaster," she said furiously, slamming the door behind her.

He laughed. "What difference does the plaster make?"

"Well, at least I could have pedalled off some of my aggression." She glowered at him and then felt guilty for making him the butt of her ill humour. "Some puke from the Regional Crime Squad is taking over my office as well as my case," she exploded. "Ten a.m. this morning. I'm to clear my desk."

Mike raised his eyebrows.

"Colclough," she explained. "Rang last night, late."

"I see." Mike was silent for a moment then, "Perhaps," he suggested, "you can work with this guy from the RCS." He ducked when a withering glance was directed his way.

So Joanna's first hour at work that morning was spent hurling things into cupboards with as much force as she could muster limited to one hand.

Then she sat behind her new desk, in the main office area, muttering as ten o'clock approached.

Her mood was not improved when 'the puke from the Regional Crime Squad' turned out to be a thin rod of a woman named Pugh, complete with stick-like legs, a sly face, pale eyes and a moustache. She walked in, stared around her, then homed in on Joanna. "Piercy," she said sharply. "I'll have a word with you first. Bring your file with you."

It was a stormy detective who planted herself in front of her own desk while Pugh's pale eyes fixed on her unblinking.

"This your office?" she asked first.

Joanna nodded and Pugh turned around to stare at the view from the window. "Doesn't the brick wall irritate you?" she asked. Joanna scowled. "It used to, at first. I used to think of it as a brick wall, leading nowhere . . . "

"And now?" Pugh asked curiously.

"I know that brick wall well," Joanna said quietly. "All the patterns, each brick, the way the rain trickles down, shadows when it's sunny. I've got used to it."

Pugh shrugged before turning her attention to Selkirk's murder. It seemed she wanted to know everything about his injuries and mode of death but little about his family's lack of grief or any sort of motive. She gave

Joanna a sharp, ugly look. "Those things don't concern me," she said briskly. "It's the *modus operandi*, the weapon and the environment that I need to know about. Other details merely cloud the issue."

Her eyes were still fixed on Joanna as she sat back and scratched her upper lip. "I wonder how he got Selkirk to walk along the corridor," she mused. "All Selkirk had to do was shout out and someone would have come running."

Joanna sat still, resentful, while Pugh rolled a pen between her fingers, frowning at the typewritten notes.

Then she looked up. "Quite good, Inspector Piercy. However, I can see that you and I are looking at this case from different angles. Aren't we?"

"Are we?"

Pugh's bony hands were spread over the papers as though she were divining for something. "Photographs?" she snapped.

Joanna threw the forensic pictures on to the desk. "Here," she said and the woman's nostrils twitched as she peered at them. For a while she said nothing but studied them closely up and down, growling and clearing her throat like an excited terrier.

Then she raised her head. "Well, at least you've got some decent pictures." She conceded a second point. "Easy to see the position from which the victim was shot."

Joanna looked at her with hostile eyes.

"Have you the PM pictures?" Pugh asked. "I want to see the entrance wound."

When Joanna found them and pushed them across Pugh peered at one in particular before looking up.

"Tell me," she said. "Was it a Beretta?"

Joanna nodded and Pugh sat back, half closing her eyes.

"It's so funny," she said, muttering to herself. "They're all the same. They never vary — with anything. Same bloody gun. He always picks a forest — some patch of wasteground. A cheap copy of the Mafia." She scrutinized the picture. "You can almost tell what books the bastard's read. And every time it's a bullet right through the back of the head as though a target had been painted on the victim's neck." She glared at Joanna. "An unpleasant way to make a living, don't you think, Piercy?"

Dumbly Joanna nodded.

Pugh dropped the pictures back on to the desk with a clatter. "He makes a lot of money," she said. "More than you or I do attempting to keep some semblance of law and order in this rapidly crumbling country of ours."

Joanna stared back at her. This was her first encounter with the Regional Crime Squad. And the power of the department was making her dizzy. She nodded, almost hypnotized by the woman.

"You understand that it's tykes like this who are the most dangerous to our civilized structure? Let men like this . . . " She jabbed her finger on the close-up of the bullet hole before letting it slide over the pictures, scattering them so the full horror of Selkirk's missing face was exposed . . . "Let men like this multiply," she said, her voice soft now, like a panther's purr, "and you can say goodbye to all forms of law and order. It will be the bullet and the knife most expertly wielded that will rule. And corrupt money." She stopped. "That is why however you may hate us for invading your space," and she gave a grim laugh, "I'm afraid you need us and will continue to do so."

Joanna blinked but said nothing. Pugh had interpreted her lack of welcome correctly.

"Now do you begin to understand why it is of paramount importance that I was hauled in?"

Joanna nodded sheepishly.

"Ma'am," she asked tentatively, "do I understand that you know who shot Selkirk?"

"Oh yes." Pugh's eyes met hers quite coolly. "I know, all right." She stopped. "I knew within half an hour of being given the facts of the case. But I'm not interested in who hired him." She gave a sharp, mirthless laugh. "I'm interested in the executioner only." She sat back and closed her eyes. "I want the finger on the trigger. Someone who will pull a man from his hospital bed and drive him a couple of miles only to murder him is a grave danger to society." Pugh stopped speaking for a moment and leafed through the sheets of paper. "Fifty metres away," she read. "Brain tissue was found on the trunk of a tree fifty metres away. And I think of all the forensic evidence that's the one fact that exposes the brutality of the single small act of pulling a trigger. Someone who will do all that, just for money." She opened her eyes and stared at Joanna. "I intend to nail that man to one of those trees."

Joanna was silent. And now she remembered Colclough's words. "Out of your league, Piercy." And she knew he had been right. This was outside both her experience and her comprehension.

And silently she gave tribute, to Colclough and to Pugh. She looked curiously at the woman. "Who is he?"

"I shall have to see the ballistics study of your bullet to be absolutely sure," Pugh said. "Thank God you bothered to find it and didn't let one of your big-footed constables tread it into the earth. But I'm fairly sure that he's an old friend of mine." She stopped. "Rather fittingly a Sicilian. We've met before. He's my pigeon and I'll get him locked away for life this time." She stared at Joanna. "I'll concentrate on him. The local detail will be left to you, Inspector Piercy." Her Adam's apple bounced in her neck as she spoke. "Think you can handle it?"

Joanna nodded and gave a soft sigh of relief. The executioner was of little interest to her. A brutal act surely without intelligent motive. Done for money. It was murder done without conscience and as such of no concern to her. It was murder on a personal level that interested her. Who, out of Selkirk's friends or acquaintances, had hated him enough to want his death? And to taunt him on the very morning of that death?

She looked curiously at Pugh. "How much," she said, "how much would he have charged for his services?"

Pugh was already leafing through the files. She hardly looked up to answer. "Round about eight k is the going rate. Unless he's put his prices up."

"How are you so certain it was him?"

Now Pugh did look up, irritated, as though explaining to a child why B followed A.

"Well, there's the evidence of the gun," she said, "as well as the bullet markings. Then there's his *modus operandi*." She stopped. "I've already explained all that, the place of execution, the knotting of the wrists. This man's — Gallini's his name — his family were all fishing folk from the southern tip of Sicily. He's a proficient knotter." She picked up another of the reports. "Always best-quality nylon sailing twine. He doesn't skimp. Then there's another curious habit he has, almost a superstition. He never changes his night," she said. "Surely you must have thought it strange, abducting someone from a hospital bed when another night the man would be a much easier target." She gave a twisted smile. "He is also a very mean man. And times are hard, even for men of his profession. If Selkirk had died of natural cases he would have lost 8k. Money Gallini could ill afford to do without with so many of his family dependent on his earnings. He couldn't afford to wait. The man was ill. Gallini's no doctor, but even with his peanut for a brain he may have realized his victim might die before he could glean his earnings from him. And once he's decided to hit on

155

a Monday or a Tuesday nothing will deter him. His family all pray for his safety on that particular night, you see." She paused. "Most people would have waited until Selkirk was home again. But Gallini was prepared to take chances, hit him in the hospital." Her face was grim. "He'll have spent half the day casing the joint, unseen by anyone."

"But . . ." Joanna objected.

"Unseen," Pugh said positively. "Who looks at a plumber, a porter, a doctor wearing a convincing identity card — or a grieving relative? He's a professional. He'll have been all these. No one will have noticed him." She picked up the photograph of the blood-stained door. "Do you know what sort of fingerprint this is?"

It was a grainy, regular surface.

"A glove?" Joanna ventured.

"Go on."

"A rubber glove."

"A bloody surgeon's glove," Pugh said triumphantly. "And that is Gallini all over. In a hospital he uses a surgeon's glove."

A thought was beginning to tempt Joanna. "Could that have been the reason Selkirk walked with Gallini along the corridor without raising the alarm?"

Pugh sat quite still for a moment, then nodded. "It's possible," she said quietly. "I'm not totally convinced. Something not quite right here. A weak spot in the planning." And she shook her head. "Gallini doesn't like weak spots, but it might have been like that." She stopped. "However, the final clincher and the thing that'll hang him, metaphorically speaking," she added hastily, "is the gun."

She leafed through the papers. "Where is the sodding ballistics report?"

"It takes at least five days," Joanna said coldly.

"We'll see about that." Pugh picked up the phone and barked some orders down it. Then she looked up. "Beretta," she said. "Typical bloody Italian. Superstitious as hell. Clever enough to use a surgeon's glove in a hospital and stupid enough to use the same gun, every bloody time."

Beside her Joanna felt a beginner.

"And he always shoots his victim in the same place," Pugh muttered. "Same range. He pushes the gun in so far you actually get a slightly smaller bore because he's puckered the skin. A moment's discomfort. Instant death. Back of the brain."

She picked up Matthew's PM report. "Nice thorough job your pathologist does. Knows what he's about, doesn't he?"

Joanna nodded and felt unbelievably proud.

Matthew was — besides all other things — also a professional.

But for now she had her own concerns. "So is it all right," she said awkwardly, "if I continue with my own investigations?"

Pugh hardly glanced up. "Do what you like," she said. "But don't even think of obstructing me. Start with a man's nearest and dearest before you move to his trusted business partners and beneficiaries from his will. And then take a look at his criminal history before looking anywhere else. OK?" Her face twisted again into an excuse for a smile. "I gather Selkirk and his unsavoury partner were being investigated by the Fraud Squad." She held up her hand. "No more details yet."

At last there was something Joanna knew more about. "Yes," she said. "Fraudulent claims for legal aid."

Pugh looked unimpressed. "Oh, that old game?"

There was one thing still puzzling Joanna. "And the letter?"

Pugh frowned. "That's totally out of character. All the rest I can picture Gallini's hand behind. But not that." She stared at Joanna. "That," she said, "was the hand that signed the cheque."

Joanna made the sign of the triumphant fist as she approached Mike's desk. "We can carry on," she said softly, her eyes trained on the closed door. "She's only interested in the killer. Not the person who paid the bill. So, I suggest we take a little drive. Visit Wilde."

Mike rattled the car keys and grinned.

Two minutes later the door flew open. "I want to see the stiff."

They both groaned.

"You . . . Korpanski. You can drive me."

On her way out Pugh tossed another line over her shoulder. "And you, Piercy. I want the doors."

Joanna stared. "But it's a hospital fire door," she said. "We got the prints. All the prints. All photographed."

"You've cordoned them off?"

"Yes."

"Then I want the bloody door," Pugh said and left the station with Mike, leaving Joanna fuming.

* * *

After a fruitless morning struggling with the SOC officers taking the door off its hinges,

Joanna called on Colclough.

"I want Mike back," she said. "I need him to drive me around. I can't do anything without him. I'm stuck, sir, with this plaster on my arm." It was itching unbearably.

He was unsympathetic. "Don't hassle me, Piercy," he groaned.

"I must have him, sir, if I'm going to proceed with the case."

"But Pugh . . ."

"I've got my own investigations," she said, "with Pugh's blessing."

"All right," he grunted. "You can have him back in the morning."

"But this afternoon . . . ?"

"Carry on your investigations here," he said, "then go home. You can have Korpanski back tomorrow."

So Joanna sat at the desk, toying one-handed with a pencil, her mind shuffling through the case. Maybe she should look deeper into this business with the Fraud Squad. There might be some clue there. And then there was that mention of an old firearms case, eight to ten years ago. Could there be a connection? She stared into space. A quick check could soon be run. But the facts didn't fit. The gunner who had polished Selkirk off had been hired. Someone hadn't wanted to get their

160

hands dirty but had preferred to part with a great deal of money. What sort of a person? Someone squeamish? Or someone with such a good reason for wanting Selkirk dead they had not dared come under the umbrella of suspicion? Someone to whom eight thousand pounds had not seemed a very great deal of money.

Her mind was fully engaged now, concentrating on this one fact. She wanted to know more about the dead man.

She called Dawn Critchlow across. "I want you to run a search on Selkirk," she said. "See if you can come up with anything." The WPC looked at her curiously. "What sort of thing did you have in mind?"

"Anything," Joanna said. "Absolutely anything. If he broke wind in court I want to know about it. And while you're at it, Dawn, run a check on firearms cases he handled eight to ten years ago."

While Dawn was gone she pondered on the Fraud Squad's investigation. She'd already studied the preliminary report. The racket had been worth hundreds of thousands of pounds through multiple claims, all costing the country through the Legal Aid system. Selkirk and Wilde had merrily robbed the nation for their own profits. She flicked through the file. Divorces and defences had formed the bulk of the claims. Practically every case they had handled was now under scrutiny. It was a thick file and it went back more than five years.

But why had Selkirk needed all that money? He had a home, a wife, cars, no dependents. His was a well-paid job yielding a steady income. Why had he needed so much more? Was it simple greed? Had the upright pillar of society a dark side to him — a cocaine habit? Joanna rejected that idea and toyed with another. Perhaps the money had been a side product and the real thrill had been nothing more than beating the very system that had financed his career.

She half closed her eyes and conjured up the photograph of Jonathan Selkirk. She pictured his direct gaze, the cynical, twisted smile, small, calculating eyes, toothbrush moustache. It had been a dry, humourless face with something conceited and conde-scending in it. Such a man would derive pleasure from cheating the system. And if that was the case, what about his partner? What had Rufus Wilde gleaned from the cheats and deals? Was his motive the pleasure of deception too, or greed?

Joanna dropped the papers across the desk. Selkirk and Wilde were intelligent men. Surely they must have realized they would eventually be found out? Or had the habit been too difficult to stop?

She glanced at her watch. Three o'clock, that midway point in the afternoon. Without Mike something was missing. She stood up. Tomorrow they would pay their visit to Rufus Wilde. But for now her arm was hurting. It was only three days since her accident. Maybe it was a delayed response to the anaesthetic, but she felt a lack of enthusiasm for working to the end of the afternoon. She was tired. Matthew was otherwise engaged. She would take the rest of the afternoon off. One of the squad cars was going towards Cheddleton. It proved easy to cadge a lift home.

★ ★ ★

Videos have their uses. In a cupboard full of old films Joanna found one that suited her mood, then lay down on the sofa with a glass of French red wine . . . She closed her eyes . . .

And was roused from a deep sleep by a brisk knock. It was dark outside. She lay for a while, confused. It wouldn't be Matthew. Not tonight. Tom?

She crossed the room and peered through the window. The knock came again, impatient this time.

In the moonlight she could just pick out a cloud of familiar pale hair and she flung open the door.

"Caro . . . Caro." She hugged her friend. "What are you doing up here? You couldn't have come at a better time."

"I wondered whether you'd be in."

"You're staying with Tom?"

Her friend gave her a warm, rocking hug. "It is good to see you," she said. "And, yes, I am staying with Tom. Darling, faithful, loving Tom. I'd be stuck without him. And as for what I'm doing here. Do you want the official version or the unofficial?"

"Both."

"Well . . . " Her friend sat down. "Tom told me about your accident." She looked at Joanna severely. "You should take more care."

"Maybe it wasn't my fault."

"Well," Caro glanced at her arm, "I wanted to see you, make certain you were OK."

"And?" Joanna said suspiciously.

"There's a story to cover," Caro said smoothly. "And I begged the editor to make it mine." She grinned. "Rather a nasty little case, isn't it?" She was watching Joanna very carefully for signs that she was brushing with the truth. "Blameless country solicitor with

a heart condition gets a hole in the head?"
She looked shrewdly at Joanna. "Or was he
quite so blameless?"

Joanna gave a helpless gesture. "Come on,
Caro," she said. "You know I can't discuss
these things."

Caro sat down, crossed her long, slim legs
and leaned against the back of the sofa. "I
suppose I could always call on the wife," she
said. "Play the old game of bluff . . . "

"I'll give you just a few things," Joanna
said. "As you're my friend. And, yes, you can
use them." She drew in a deep breath. "The
Regional Crime Squad have been called
in."

Caro's eyes flickered.

"They believe a known assassin, available
for hire, shot Jonathan Selkirk."

Caro's eyebrows shot up. "Name?"

But Joanna made the same quick gesture
with her hands. "No name," she said. "But
I'm confident he'll be brought to trial. Fairly
quickly."

"Good." Caro scribbled in her quick,
angular shorthand. "Anything else?"

"We-ell — and I can't give you details
on this — Selkirk and Wilde were under
investigation by the Fraud Squad."

Caro smiled. "Great. Just great."

"Now perhaps you'll put the kettle on,"

Joanna said drily. "It's a bit difficult with my arm in plaster."

Caro disappeared into the kitchen and returned a few minutes later carrying two cups of coffee.

She halted in front of the table and saw the square box with its fancy wrapping paper. "Wedding present, Joanna?" Her eyes were wide and warm. She came and sat by her friend.

"Oh, darling, you're getting married. And you didn't even tell me. What a traitor you can be."

"We're *not* getting married. Matthew's bought me a crash helmet."

Caro was always quick to pick up undercurrents. Her eyes narrowed. "I see," she said, then glanced around the room. "And where is Matthew tonight?"

Joanna drank her coffee. "Jane's wielding her secret weapon," she said sourly.

Caro looked at her friend quizzically.

"Matthew isn't here," she said, "because he's with Jane tonight."

"Mmmm." Caro looked sceptical.

"Eloise is playing the flute in a school concert," Joanna said flatly. "Eloise is Jane's secret weapon. Whenever she thinks Matthew and I are in danger of forgetting he already has a wife she plays the Eloise card. You know," she said bitterly. "*You have a daughter. Do not neglect.* And Matthew's so riddled with guilt he does triple somersaults to prove he's not neglectful."

"Hmm," Caro said again. "And how are you getting on with young Miss Eloise?"

"She dislikes me just about as much as it is possible to dislike anyone," Joanna said. "And of course that keeps Jane very happy. Matthew only ever sees Eloise on his own. Never with me. So I don't see her. It's early days yet," she said in defence.

Caro's all-seeing, intelligent eyes were trained on her face. "Seems to me," she said perceptively, "that it isn't just Matthew who suffers from guilt." Her face grew angular and sharp. "And that's not all, is it, Joanna? I know you, there's something else."

Joanna frowned, pushing back other fears — fears she had never voiced, even to Matthew. But the day was coming when she would be forced to confront them. She stared helplessly at her friend.

"Come on," Caro said gently, "tell me."

Joanna gave a deep sigh. "It's very muddled. I don't know if I'll be able to put it across very well."

"Try me."

"Well . . . when Matthew left his wife and daughter," Joanna said, frowning, "I know they weren't very happy." She stopped. "But I know too that however unhappy he was at home he would have stayed if it hadn't been for me."

"And yet you're still living apart," Caro observed. "Six months after he finally left her."

Joanna nodded and found words even more difficult. "I think," she began. "I think what he wants and what I want are just poles apart. He wants — commitment . . . another home. Once or twice he's mentioned children." And now she had actually said it it was a relief. She knew just how much this had been upsetting her.

"I think he expects me to be a wife."

"And what do you want?"

"I *don't* want to be a housewife," she said. "I want to carry on being a cop."

"Part time?"

Joanna shook her head. "No," she said. "The full commitment . . . the whole lot. Policing's more than a full-time job. It's wherever and whenever you're needed. I haven't got time to be a wife."

"And?"

"I don't want children," Joanna said. "I don't ever want children."

Caro leaned back on the sofa. "Oh dear."

"The trouble is . . . " Tears were pricking

Joanna's lids. "I have the awful feeling that if I'm honest with Matthew he'll go home, back to Jane." She stopped. "He doesn't really like living in his flat, alone. He's pushing me to sell this place and for us to get married, buy a home, and all the rest of the package." She gave a low laugh. "So I'm sitting here on my hands, trying to buy time." She stood up suddenly. "But it's borrowed time, Caro, and I know it."

9

Matthew didn't ring that night or the following morning, but by now she had learned the pattern. In a day or two he would reappear. Jane's beseeching and Eloise's tears always left Matthew confused and guilty. So he never came straight back to her but took a day or two to recover.

And Joanna spent yet another sleepless night; but it was the precursor to a fruitful day, the most productive since Selkirk's murder.

Mike called at eight thirty, a wide grin on his face. "I don't know what you said to Colclough," he chirped, "but I'm seconded back to you and Pugh's got one of the uniformed lads."

"Excellent," Joanna said. And that was just the beginning of her day's luck.

During the car journey she told Mike her thoughts from the day before and appreciated his quiet attention, especially when she enlarged on the investigation by the Fraud Squad.

"It's been a big venture," she said, "much bigger than I'd realized. Though why Selkirk needed more money beats me."

"Expensive tastes?"

"Maybe." She cast him a swift glance before adding, "I'm glad to have you back, Mike. I can think better when you're around."

His neck turned puce. "I suppose I'd better look on the bright side," he replied gruffly. "Things could have been worse. I could have had her for a colleague instead of you. The thought of doing the midnight watch with that moustache . . . " He gave a bovine laugh.

"Watch it," she warned. "If I thump you with this plaster you'll know all about it."

The second bit of luck that day was waiting for her in the main office.

Dawn Critchlow was standing by her desk. "Surprise, surprise, Inspector," she said. "I didn't expect anything to come up on the search. But the computer found Selkirk did have a criminal record. Apart from the Fraud Squad investigation."

Joanna looked at her. "Really?"

WPC Critchlow nodded. "He was involved in a fatal road accident. Five years ago he knocked down and killed a little girl on a school crossing." She stopped. "He seriously injured the lolly lady, too. She lost both legs. It was all rather horrible. The little girl died

171

on the road, watched by her school friends. Her injuries were pretty horrific, according to the post-mortem. I remember the case quite well. I just hadn't realized it was the same man. It happened during the lunchbreak. The girl had been home for her dinner and was returning to school when the accident happened."

Joanna sensed there was more. "Go on," she said.

"Selkirk didn't stop, he drove on. There were lots of people around and they took his number and got a description too." She hesitated. "The feeling amongst police and the general public was that Selkirk had been way over the legal alcohol limit at the time of the accident. He'd been out to lunch with friends. They all swore he had only had two single whiskies. He was picked up an hour after the accident, at home, swigging from a bottle. Of course the prosecution could not prove . . . " she made a face, " . . . beyond reasonable doubt that he had been over the limit at the time of the accident." He had a very good solicitor who put the case forward that his client had been so upset by the accident that he had been frozen, unable to stop. Trauma denial, he called it. And it fooled the court. But it didn't fool anybody else connected with the case. There were

172

riots outside when the verdict was given and most of the following day when Selkirk was sentenced.

"He was charged with leaving the scene of an accident. A fine and suspended sentence." She frowned. "There were nearly charges of affray . . . The relatives actually made death threats."

She looked at Joanna. "This is the bit I think you'll find particularly interesting. They sent him letters. Anonymous letters warning him. Some of them were still on file." She bit her lip. "Written on a word processor, on A4 paper, no heading. One of them advised him to make will."

Joanna sat down open-mouthed. "To make a will?"

She gave Mike a triumphant glance.

"Well," she said. "This looks like as strong a motive as any. Thanks, Dawn, you've done really well." She paused. "Have you actually seen the letters?"

"There were photocopies of them on file, and superficially they looked the same."

"We'd better go and visit these people, Mike."

"There is one thing," Dawn put in reluctantly. "It's about the letter. The child's family was given a warning, unofficially. They were pretty sick about the whole matter. And no charges were ever brought. But after that the letters stopped. That was three years ago, and there hasn't been a single one since. So why now?"

They looked at each other and Joanna shrugged her shoulders. "We'll have to climb that gate when we meet it," she said. "What was the little girl's name?"

"Rowena Carter," Dawn replied. "The family still live in the same house. Emily Place, number fourteen. It's on the new housing estate."

"We'll call round there now."

Mike interrupted. "What about Wilde?"

"He can wait," Joanna said. "We'll see him this afternoon. I think Rowena Carter's family lie a little nearer the truth."

★ ★ ★

Emily Place was part of a neat new development built about five years previously. When Rowena Carter died the house must have been almost new. They pulled up outside and Joanna stared at the polished picture window and tidy flowerbeds. A car stood in the drive, a four-year-old Vauxhall. All looked cared for and in order. But unlike the other drives on the estate there were no bikes lying around, no colourful plastic toys.

No sandpit, no child-proof gate. Perhaps, Joanna thought, it was all a little too orderly. Maybe it could have benefited from just a tiny touch of chaos.

"A difficult interview to open," she mused. Mike nodded.

"Come on, then," and they walked up the path and knocked on the door.

A man in his late twenties pulled open the door, medium height, wearing a vest and jeans. His shoulders were heavily tattooed with dragons and a mermaid. His head was shaved almost bald. One gold sleeper was threaded through his right earlobe.

He looked at Joanna, then at Mike, and his face flushed. "I can guess who you are," he said. "Written all over you." He stood back to let them enter. "I had the feeling you'd come."

"You're Mr Carter?"

His face was puffed, lined and unhappy, older than his years. He had the look of a drinker. "Who else would I be?"

"I'm Detective Inspector Piercy and this is Detective Sergeant Korpanski," Joanna said. "You expected us?"

Carter nodded and his mouth twisted again. "Time was," he said, "when I'd have done that gladly, and gone to prison for it too. I won't pretend I weren't glad."

He turned and they followed him into a neat but small lounge-dining room with a polished teak table at one end and a three-piece suite, television and video at the other. Five portraits hung over the gas fire and one empty hook. The sixth was missing. And they were all of the same dark-haired, pretty, laughing child.

Carter followed their gaze. "Yes," he said. "That's her. That's our little Row."

And Joanna felt suddenly inadequate. "You have other children, Mr Carter?"

The man wiped his hand across his face. "Ann was pregnant when he killed our Rowena," he said. "She lost 'im an' all." His voice was tough, unemotional and tightly controlled. "We gave up then. Didn't seem like we was meant to have kids. They was taken away."

Joanna glanced at Mike then back at Mr Carter. She was still at a loss for words.

"The anger'll never leave me," he said. "Not me nor Ann. We're empty because of 'im. Like old people with nothin' to say. What's 'e left us? Bugger all."

They were silent and Carter continued. "If the law had let us have what was right, if they'd have locked 'im up, put 'im away — something — it wouldn't 'ave bin so bad.

As it was they just took his side."

"As I understand it," Joanna said cautiously, "it couldn't be proved that Selkirk was drunk at the time of the accident."

Carter gave her a withering look. "Everyone in that whole court knew," he said bitterly. "Everyone — even the judge. I could see it in his eyes. He knew Selkirk and that smart solicitor chap what was defending him. They all knew. But they couldn't do anything." Suddenly he stopped and smiled, and his face was transformed.

"Do you want to see something pretty?"

They both nodded because they didn't know what else to say or do.

"Come up here, then." And they followed him upstairs.

It was a tiny landing, no more than a yard square of blue carpet. Four doors led off it. On one of them was a ceramic plaque. Rowena's Room, it said. And the writing was embellished by a long-stemmed, deep red rose.

Carter pushed the door wide open. Inside, strewn across the floor, were little girls' toys. All the favourites. Cindy's house, Barbie's car. My Little Pony. A pair of small red leather sandals was tucked underneath the bed, their straps hanging undone. A multi-coloured quilt covered the bed. The window was ajar and the curtains blew gently in the breeze. The scent of fragrant, little girl's talcum powder still hung in the air. Joanna looked all the way around the room, then back at Carter. His eyes were moist.

"It's a lovely room, isn't it?" he said.

Joanna nodded.

"We got Rowena to stay at her gran's one weekend," he said, "and then we bombed down to the cash-and-carry and got this wallpaper. It were a bargain. By the time little Row got home Sunday night we'd done the lot."

He rubbed his eyes with his bare, tattooed arm. "Ann done the quilt, while I painted and put the paper on the walls. Row was that excited when she got 'ome she got straight into bed." He laughed. "It were only four o'clock in the afternoon."

"You've kept the room like this?"

Carter nodded. "She 'as an 'eadstone," he said, "with 'er name on. But it's in the churchyard. It don't seem like 'er somehow." He frowned painfully. "She loved pretty things, did our Row. So 'ere" — he glanced lingeringly around the room — "it's 'er," he said slowly. "It's like she's still in here." He stopped. "You can still smell 'er, can't you?"

He looked at Joanna. "What would you do

if someone made one of your kids suffer?" His face was frozen with hatred. "In pieces, she were," he said brokenly. "In pieces. Bits of 'er on the road." He couldn't contain the grief now. "Me and Ann, we thought we 'ad it made. I 'ad a job — a good one, solid too. We bought this place. Then little Row, and another on the way. What right," he said fiercely, "what bloody right did that bastard Selkirk have to take it all away?"

Downstairs Carter offered them tea and they accepted. These questions would not be rushed. Carter handed the mugs round and offered them both sugar.

"Your wife isn't at home?" Joanna began conversationally.

Carter glanced at his watch. "She'll be here in a minute. She's only at the school."

"I thought you didn't have any more children."

"We haven't," he said shortly.

"She works there?"

Carter shook his head. "Drop it," he said, suddenly vicious. "Ask your questions if you 'ave to then bugger off. Just leave us alone. We know fuck all about Selkirk's murder, but *I'd* like to ask *you* one thing."

She waited.

"I want to meet the bloke that forced that bastard to kneel and made him beg

179

for mercy." He swallowed. "Because I'd like to shake 'im by the hand."

Joanna hardly dared breathe. She gave Mike a swift glance and read the question in his eyes.

How had Carter known that Jonathan Selkirk had been forced to kneel? The story in the papers had reported the place and circumstances of the killing but the police had specifically asked them to omit that Selkirk had been forced to his knees.

"We will have to speak to your wife too," she insisted. "The sooner the better."

"As you want," Carter grunted.

"Mr Carter, did you have anything to do with Mr Selkirk's murder?"

Carter shook his head. "No, I didn't."

Joanna watched him carefully. But even with this morning's new knowledge she had not expected a simple confession.

"Do you know Gallows Wood, Mr Carter?"

He nodded. "I've been there once or twice."

"For what reason?"

Carter's face was screwed up. "Just walking," he said. "Just getting out of the house."

"When were you last there?"

"Couple of months ago." Carter stood up, agitated, and peered out of the polished

180

window. "Do you want to know where my wife is, Inspector?"

And Joanna had a horrid, creeping feeling. She already knew.

"Every bloody morning, dinner time, teatime." His voice stabbed at the words. "She stands on that bloody school crossing, every day, in the middle of the flipping road, helping the kids to cross. And do you know what she's praying?" He didn't even wait for her to ponder. "She's praying some other drunken psychopath will plough into her the way it did to our little girl. Now do you understand me? I didn't kill Selkirk. But I'm glad if he suffered. He deserved to." The muscles at the side of his mouth twitched. "He sent us a bloody cheque after killin' Rowena. Five hundred pound." His face twisted with a furious grief. "That's when I started sending him the letters. I couldn't stomach it."

Carter looked at Mike. "He's ruined our lives. And there's Molly. She lost her legs. So if Selkirk's dead it's no more than he deserved. Unfortunately I haven't got a gun."

Joanna leaned forward and set down her mug on the small polished wine table. "You wouldn't have needed a gun," she said. "The person who actually shot Selkirk," she spoke in a low voice, "was in all probability paid to do it."

"What? A hired killer?" Carter looked astounded. "You mean someone paid another person to kill Selkirk?" He scratched his head. That's a new one on me. Well, that's me off the hook, then, I wouldn't 'ave robbed myself of the pleasure. I would 'ave done it myself, if I'd 'ave thought I could get away with it."

"Would you?"

Slowly Carter nodded." If you'd 'ave been through what me and my wife 'ave for the last five years, you'd understand." He rubbed his arms as though he were cold. "Bugger me. So it wasn't just us what hated him. There was others."

He paused at the sound of a key grating in the front door and a woman walked in. She glanced at her husband. "Police?" she asked and he nodded.

She was thin with a pale face and untidy hair dressed in black leggings and a long, black sweater. Over her arm she carried a plastic, fluorescent yellow coat. Pinned to her sweater was a brooch the size of a hen's egg containing a picture of the same dark-haired, pretty, laughing child.

She flopped down in the seat and sat, staring at them with a bitter smile. "So you think it was us, do you?"

Joanna started to speak. "We're investigating all — " but the woman interrupted her.

"We did have reason." She pushed a handful of hair out of her tired eyes. "But we didn't have anything to do with Selkirk's miserable death. Justice is done, in the end." Her mouth tightened. "Just tell me he suffered," she said bitterly. "Tell me he suffered."

Joanna looked away, startled. She fished in her bag and produced Selkirk's final threatening letter. "Did you send this," she asked.

Ann Carter studied it, then frowned and shook her head. "No," she said. "It looks the same as one of ours. But we didn't." She glanced at her husband. "We stopped after the police told us, didn't we?"

Her husband hesitated before giving a slow, trusting nod.

Mike was watching her curiously. "Did you say it looks like the letters you used to send?"

"It does," she said. "It's uncanny, really." She glanced again at the copy of the letter in Mike's hand. "It's just the same."

Joanna decided to throw caution to the wind. "Does the name Gallini mean anything to you?" she asked.

Both Carters shook their heads.

183

They were in the car before Joanna felt it was safe to speak. "What do you think, Mike?"

He was watching the neat, sad house as he turned the car round. "They've got to be our hottest suspects so far."

"But why wait? Rowena died five years ago. They last sent a letter three years ago."

"Maybe," he said flippantly, "they needed to save up. Eight thousand pounds is a lot of money."

"Yes," she said thoughtfully. "Yes it is."

10

Selkirk & Wilde proved to be a square, stone Georgian house in the middle of the town. It looked every inch a prosperous business premises with its arched portico and nine-paned windows neatly painted black. The brass plate held only two names: Jonathan Selkirk and Rufus Wilde.

Inside, a neat blonde sat at an antique mahogany desk. Dressed in a tailored black suit that somehow combined mourning with elegance, she rose as they entered, efficiently took their names and spoke into the intercom. "It's the police." Her voice was awed, hushed.

The door opened.

Had Joanna been forced to imagine a fraudulent solicitor she would never have dreamed up Wilde. Because he looked every inch the traditional professional, old school tie and Establishment. Even his gold-rimmed glasses were somehow reassuring.

"Detective Inspector Piercy and Detective Sergeant Korpanski." Joanna performed the introductions.

Wilde's eyes flickered over her plaster.

Politely he said nothing but gave a great, heaving sigh that encompassed both her broken wrist and his partner's murder.

"A dreadful business this," he said, fingering his black tie.

"As you say, Mr Wilde. A dreadful business."

"Do you have any idea . . . ?" His voice trailed away.

Behind him the blonde sat down. Wilde addressed her. "Tea please, darling." He gave Mike and Joanna a wicked wink. "My daughter," he explained. "Keeping it in the family. Wilde's glasses glinted as he turned and caught the light.

"Let's make ourselves comfortable," he said genially and led them through the door into the inner sanctum — a dark, luxurious room panelled in oak.

Once they were all seated in the deep buttoned leather-covered armchairs he returned to his original question. "Do you have any idea who might have done it?"

"No," Joanna said cautiously. "At least, we've plenty of ideas. But nothing definite, not yet."

"I see." Wilde relaxed back into his chair, steepled his fingertips together and smiled. "Now what can I do for you?"

"How long had you and Jonathan Selkirk

been in partnership, Mr Wilde?"

"Almost twenty years," he said mournfully. "It was a long time. I never guessed it would end so tragically. You don't, do you?"

"How did you think it would end?" Mike was sounding irritable. "In jail?"

Wilde's eyes flickered dangerously behind the glasses and he cleared his throat, shifted in his chair.

"Look, Sergeant whatever-your-name-is, I'm under investigation by the Fraud Squad. I'm not trying to deny it." He met Mike's eyes fearlessly. "But in this country that still means I — and this company — are innocent."

"Until proved guilty?" Mike's voice was as rough as sandpaper. "Innocent like when he ran that little girl down on the crossing?"

"That was nothing to do with me."

"But you were one of the people he had been in the restaurant with, weren't you?"

"Do your homework, Sergeant," Wilde snapped. "I was nowhere near."

Mike jerked back in his chair.

"And as far as the Fraud Squad goes," Wilde said smoothly, "I continue to protest my innocence, however much you may attempt to bully me." He gave a swift glance at Joanna. "Yes, as a criminal solicitor I am well aware of the brutal tactics of the police." He sat forward and thumped his fists on the desk. "But you won't bully me. I . . . "

"Don't tell me," Joanna said wearily. "You know your rights. Look," she said. "I'm not interested in your alleged fraudulent dealings except where they relate to this case. You're under investigation and that's enough for me. My sole purpose in coming here today is to try to find out, first of all, whether your partner telephoned you from the hospital on Monday night. If he did, did he say anything that might have a bearing on his murder? Secondly, I want to know of anyone you know who hated him enough to want him dead."

Wilde relaxed, settled back again in his chair. "In answer to your first question. Yes, Jonathan did telephone me from the hospital."

"May I ask what about?"

Wilde pursed his lips. "He knew he was ill. Very ill. He was worried about a couple of cases he was managing. He asked me to take them over." He grinned wolfishly. "You see? Nothing very murky at all."

Joanna stared at him. "Did he say anything that might illuminate the events of Monday night?"

Wilde shook his head regretfully. "No," he said. "Nothing."

"Was he concerned about his condition?"

"Not unduly." It was obvious from Wilde's brief answers that he had decided if he must co-operate he would be as unhelpful as possible.

"He had received a threatening letter that morning," Joanna said. "Did he mention it?"

Wilde sat frozen for a moment before deciding which answer to give. "He knew who the letter was from," he said. "And he asked me to take action against the people concerned."

"He thought it was from the Carters?"

Wilde nodded. "I see, Inspector, you've been doing your homework."

She brushed the sarcasm aside. "Mr Wilde, I have to tell you. The Carters deny having sent that letter."

Wilde looked astounded. "But Jonathan was convinced it was from them. He told me it was another — exactly the same as before — and would I please see to it."

"And what did that mean — 'see to it'?"

Wilde shifted his gaze back to Mike. "I took it to mean, Sergeant, that he wanted me to warn them off with a letter." He opened the top drawer. "I'd actually dictated one . . . " he held out a small audio cassette, "before I heard Jonathan's body had been found."

"What did you think had happened to him at first, when he was missing?"

Wilde contemplated for a while, staring up at the ceiling. "To be honest, I thought he'd had some sort of a brainstorm, a breakdown. I imagined him wandering somewhere. He really had been under a lot of pressure in recent months."

"Anything we should know about?"

Wilde leaned forward confidingly. "I don't things were all that wonderful at home. Sheila Selkirk," he said with a frown and a headshake. "Very strange lady, you know. And then there was this wretched investigation. Your colleagues in the Fraud Squad are none too polite, Inspector, and they make their presence felt." He looked hopefully at Joanna. "Do you think they might drop the investigation now that Jonathan's dead?"

She stared at him. The hope in his words lit his entire face. "I don't know," she said slowly. "I wouldn't have thought so. After all, Mr Wilde, you were *both* under investigation."

"Selkirk & Wilde was under investigation," he said crossly. "And the firm no longer exists. You can't take action against the dead."

"But you can against the living, Mr Wilde."

He was biting his lip. "I know that."

But the exchange had given Joanna a focus for her thoughts. Surely Rufus Wilde could not have been naive enough to believe he could shift all the blame on to his partner — now deceased?

But as she watched the solicitor fingering his dark tie she dismissed this as a motive. It was almost certainly too flimsy. Yet the doubt remained and she watched his movements with a heightened curiosity.

"Who wanted your partner dead, Mr Wilde?"

"No one," he said earnestly. "Absolutely no one in the entire world. Jonathan was a first-class man. Popular. Loved by all who knew him." He paused for breath. "He had the respect — the greatest respect — of every single person in Leek who had professional dealings with him."

It was as false an epitaph as any Joanna had heard.

"Even the criminals he prosecuted?"

Wilde gave a bland smile. "Just doing his job."

Joanna tried a new tack. "Mrs Selkirk mentioned a firearms case after which Mr Selkirk was threatened."

"And when would this have been?" Wilde touched the side of his glasses.

"Eight to ten years ago," Mike said.

Wilde's face was impassive as he thought. "Ah, yes. That would have been the Wilton case. Certainly he made some threats but he didn't mean business. It was all sabre-rattling."

The veins on Mike's neck were standing out like ropes. "Sure about that, are you?"

"Oh, yes." Wilde's tone was condescending. "You can always tell."

"Still around, is he, this Mr Wilton?"

"I really couldn't tell you."

"So you can't think of anyone else who disliked Jonathan Selkirk?"

"No."

"Not even his son?"

"Absolutely not," Wilde said, "though I have to say Justin was a grave disappointment to his father."

"Why is that?"

"Intellectually, you know. Jonathan had hoped Justin would follow him into the profession. Despite good schooling the boy showed no interest. No interest at all."

"A shame." But Mike's sarcasm was wasted on the pompous solicitor.

Joanna stood up. "Thank you, Mr Wilde. We'll be in touch."

It was the last phrase that seemed to rattle Wilde more than anything else. He stared at her with a flicker of fear in his eyes. Was the impending fraud investigation so threatening to him? Or was this the result of a guilty conscience. But why? Why on earth might he have wanted his partner dead?

She was almost through the door when the neat blonde returned with a tray of white porcelain tea cups, smothered in pink roses and a large, steaming tea pot.

"Sorry, love," Mike said. "Too late." Then he turned back to face Wilde. "I hope they'll ask you to give the speech at Selkirk's funeral. You give by far the best one. Everyone else," he finished, "seems to have hated his guts."

★ ★ ★

On return to the station Joanna was met by Dawn Critchlow. "Which do you want first?" she asked. "The good news, the news or the bad news?"

"Oh, the good, always the good," Joanna said.

"Dr Levin phoned. He mentioned dinner tonight and says would you ring back to confirm." She smiled. "He wants to book."

Joanna's eyes flickered. If Matthew wanted to book a table it meant a serious talk. She had avoided confrontation with him for as long as was possible. She knew what was coming, had always known. Matthew always broke bad news face to face.

She pushed the thoughts to the back of her mind. "The news?"

"A car was spotted in the lay-by near Gallows Wood at one thirty a.m. approx. A Vauxhall Cavalier, brown. And the person even got the number. We've checked it out."

"And?"

"Holloway," Dawn said. "It's owned by someone called Dustin Holloway. We'll run some checks on him."

"Good."

"Who called in?" Joanna asked idly. "Courting couple?"

Dawn Critchlow nodded. "Wouldn't you guess? Both married to other people so they didn't come forward earlier."

Joanna turned to Mike. "We'd better check our obliging witnesses out," she said, "as well as this Holloway. And the bad news?" she said to Dawn.

"Pugh wants you in her — sorry, *your* — office the minute you walk in. Sorry," she said again. "But that was how she worded it. If I were you," she winked at Mike, "I should talk to Dr Levin first."

Joanna dropped her eyes and sighed. Somehow even Pugh seemed preferable to Matthew just at the moment.

Pugh was no more attractive on their second meeting. Her pale eyes looked up as Joanna entered.

"I shall be vacating your office late this evening," she said sharply. "Gallini's been picked up."

So quickly? Joanna thought. "Where?" she said aloud.

"Heathrow. With a pocketful of money, waiting to board a plane to Sicily, ready for a family holiday and taking the money back to Papa Mafioso."

"Any chance of him talking?"

"I doubt it. But I do have something else for you. Sit down, Piercy."

Joanna dropped obediently into the chair.

"I always wondered," Pugh began, "how they got Selkirk to get out of bed having ripped off all his machines, and then how they got him to drip his bloody way along the corridor and leave the relative safety of the hospital without his calling out." She stared at Joanna. "I was never very happy about that."

Joanna waited.

"You may be a big fish here in a small Staffordshire town, Piercy, but you still have a lot to learn. An examination was done on the door. Fire doors," she said simply, "have to be opened from the inside."

"We knew that."

Pugh shook her head. "So he had to have a helper. Someone let him in."

Joanna stared.

"You must return to the hospital and speak again to the nurses on duty that night. One of them let Gallini in as well as tore off the machines."

★ ★ ★

It was more difficult to speak to Matthew. She dialled the lab twice, both times replacing the receiver before she was connected. The third time his secretary answered and put her through straight away.

"Hi, Matthew."

"Hello." His voice sounded strained. "I've been having a long think, Jo," he said slowly.

"With Jane's prompting." Her voice sounded every inch the jealous mistress.

"Please," he said with a sigh. "Darling ... don't make things so difficult." And immediately she felt guilty.

He tried again. "I must talk to you, Joanna. There's such a lot I need to say. I really do want us to stay together but we won't if you keep skirting the issues."

She knew he was right.

"I'll book a table for eight," he said, "at the Mermaid."

★ ★ ★

She found it difficult to concentrate at the afternoon's briefing. Her mind kept wandering . . . Life without Matthew? Life without her work? Life trying to juggle both? She kept hearing Matthew's voice, serious and set on a course of action. He could be a very determined character. She blinked and forced her mind to move back to the briefing and the roomful of officers who were depending on her to direct their enquiries.

"There are four main areas," she said, using the charts and a blackboard, "where we must concentrate our investigation." She drew in a deep breath. "Thanks to the agent from the Regional Crime Squad we have the man responsible for the shooting.

"As they thought, he is a Sicilian named Gallini. He's been known to be available for hire and is apparently responsible for other killings. Ballistics evidence connects him with at least three others, all shootings. His *modus operandi* was typical. Pugh thought around eight thousand pounds would have changed hands for Selkirk's death certificate." She stopped. "We don't know anything about the car he was driving. We have a sighting of a brown Vauxhall Cavalier at one thirty on the night in question. Seen by a courting couple. We'll want to run checks on them. The Cavalier belongs to a man called Dustin Holloway." She paused. "Everything's worth a try.

"Thanks to Pugh" — she ignored the ripple of derision that did a Mexican wave around the room — "*thanks to Pugh* it has been pointed out that someone from the hospital let him in. There was definitely an accomplice."

"But we thought . . . " Mike looked startled.

"There are two reasons why she came to this conclusion. Firstly she examined the sills in the adjacent hospital ward, which was empty on the night of the abduction. They gave no sign of an intruder." She glanced around the room, found two faces and smiled. "Thanks to an afternoon with Timmis and McBrine, who removed the fire door," she said, "we now know that was where Gallini entered the hospital."

She drew in breath. "The other reason why an inside accomplice was suspected is that the alarm on the cardiorator had been turned off. We're going to need a small team to look into details of the three nurses' bank accounts, personal details, any sort of area that might have bearing on possible criminal activity."

Mike touched her elbow. "What about all that fuss about the depressive who threw himself out of the window?"

"I don't know." Joanna frowned.

Mike was staring at her. "Well, you're the one who doesn't like coincidence," he pointed out.

She spoke back into the room. "The second area we wish to concentrate on is Jonathan Selkirk's business life. We already know a fraud case was hanging over Selkirk & Wilde. Interestingly, Rufus Wilde, I think, welcomed his partner's death." She made a face. "In spite of his new black tie and his daughter's mourning suit, I think he had an idea the Fraud Squad might just drop the case against them. He doesn't know the Fraud Squad."

More amusement emanated from the assembled officers.

"Another thing that makes me extra interested in Mr Wilde is that he has admitted that the phone call from the hospital was made to him." She held up her hand. "I'm not going to attempt to speculate what Selkirk had to say to his partner. Wilde claims that he was instructing him on some clients, but it could have been anything."

She glanced around the room. "Dawn, do you think you could liaise with the Fraud Squad, make sure I have all the details on Selkirk & Wilde's case, right up to today, and find out all you can about Selkirk and his neat little daughter." She frowned. "I didn't like that show of filial duty. And the black suit . . . "

"I can't see her forking out eight k to get rid of her father's business partner," Mike pointed out.

Joanna narrowed her eyes. "No, but I can see her presenting the cheque to her father — for signing."

Joanna turned back to the board. "Next," she said, "we have Selkirk's sweet little family — wife, son, daughter-in-law — and 'family friend', Anthony Pritchard. All of whom seem to positively welcome Selkirk's demise." She tutted. "I've never known a family apparently so liberated by the death of a member." She looked around the faces. "It's quite bizarre. And, needless to say, it puts the family in a very unfavourable light. Therefore, I shall be visiting Justin Selkirk and his wife as well as interviewing 'Grandpa' Tony in the next day or so.

"Then, last, we have the Carter family, who are the exact opposite of the Selkirks. They still have open sores over the death of their daughter, Rowena, who was knocked down on a school crossing by Selkirk five years ago. He abandoned the scene of the crime, thus making a later blood alcohol level of three times the legal limit inadmissible in court." She could hear the officers groaning.

"The Carters sent abusive letters to Selkirk until they were reprimanded by the police. Wilde claims that Selkirk asked him to warn the Carters off again after receiving an anonymous letter on the morning he died. Superficially, it looks like another one from the Carter family. We've sent it to forensics for analysis. They should have had time to do the comparison later today."

She looked around the room. "Wherever your sympathies lie," she said, "and we all feel appalled at the death of little Rowena Carter, this man was brutally murdered, and the law is the law."

As the officers filed out she spoke to Mike. "There are two things worrying me as far as the Carter family are concerned, Mike. One, how did they know Selkirk had been forced to kneel? It wasn't in any of the papers."

"And?"

Her face was troubled now. "Remember

the wall of their sitting room? All those photographs?"

Mike nodded.

"One was missing. I just wonder if it was used to remind someone of the Rowena Carter case."

11

Grateful to have her office back, Joanna and Mike were sitting eating sandwiches for a very late lunch and washing them down with the fifth coffee of the day when Joanna's telephone rang. It was the duty sergeant.

"You've got a visitor, ma'am."

She spoke with her mouth full. "Are you going to tell me who it is or is this a game of twenty questions?"

"He's given his name as Pritchard."

They heard the sergeant speak to someone in the background . . . "Got a first name, sir?"

"Don't worry, I know it," Joanna said drily. "Send him in."

They heard the footsteps tap smartly along the corridor before there was a rap on the door and Mike pulled it open.

"Mr Pritchard," he said in a genial voice. "How very nice of you to call in and offer to help with the case."

To give 'Grandpa Tony' his due, he wasn't taken in by Mike's friendliness but glanced nervously around the room.

"Sergeant," he said formally, "Inspector."

203

"Please," Joanna said, "do sit down."

Mike took up his customary position — arms folded, legs apart, leaning against the door.

Pritchard flopped down into the seat.

"What can we do for you, Mr Pritchard?"

"Look," he said awkwardly. "I thought I'd better come in. Explain a few things."

Joanna raised her eyebrows.

"Sheila doesn't know I'm here."

Joanna waited.

"I thought you should know a bit more about Jonathan Selkirk. It might help you to understand why he was murdered in the first place, and why his family are not exactly heartbroken." His eyes were trained on Joanna's face. "But it doesn't mean they had anything to do with it. They didn't wish him dead."

"No?"

Pritchard's mouth was working furiously. "Look — I know I was his friend . . . " He was having a hard time hunting for the right words. "But he wasn't quite what he seemed."

Who is? Joanna thought.

"He was very good at appearing the genial country solicitor." Pritchard coloured then, and looked ashamed. "His family knew him better — unfortunately."

The two police officers exchanged glances. Was Pritchard such a fool that he couldn't see what he was doing? Or was this a clumsy attempt at playing a double game? Joanna scrutinized his face. Just what was he up to?

"Really? Well, Mr Pritchard," she said blandly, "how very helpful of you." She rested her plaster cast on the desk where it looked even more cumbersome and felt more heavy than on her lap. "It's always helpful to know a bit more about the victim when you're investigating a murder."

"Yeah, nice of you to come in and talk to us," Mike echoed.

Pritchard could not help but hear the sarcasm in Mike's voice. He swivelled round, met Mike's hostile gaze and quickly turned back to face Joanna.

"Do go on, Mr Pritchard." She was finding it difficult to pronounce a judgement. Sheila Selkirk had carefully portrayed him as a friend of her and her husband both. Yet obviously this was far from the truth. So had this handsome, distinguished, rather elegant man merely waited in the wings? Possibly. Sheila Selkirk was a handsome woman. Correction — a handsome widow, handsome and now wealthy too. Pritchard was a widower. They would make a good-looking couple.

So why drop her in it?

She waited for Pritchard to enlarge on his story. He cleared his throat. "You don't know what sort of life Sheila had with him," he began. "He was an absolute tyrant. He liked control. And he drank, you know. She met him when they were both students."

Joanna nodded.

"She had a better degree than he did but he was jealous of her. He couldn't cope with having such a beautiful, intelligent wife."

Pritchard leaned forward to confide. "He never allowed her to practise law. It was a condition of their marriage. Systematically — all their life together — he eroded her self-confidence by criticism." He drew in a deep breath. "And he was mean. Do you know, Inspector, when she went to the supermarket he'd check all the way down the list for unnecessary items. She would have to justify each one and if she couldn't he reduced the amount of housekeeping the following week."

Joanna kept silent.

"And as for the way he treated Justin . . . it defied belief that any man could be so cruel to his own flesh and blood. My dear wife and I never had children of our own so I was very fond of Justin. He became like a son to us. Poor old thing, he had a terrible time at school."

Joanna regarded Pritchard steadily. "They must have been delighted when he was shot," she said conversationally.

Tony Pritchard flushed again. "I . . . "

Joanna's gaze was steely. "There is such a thing as divorce, you know, Mr Pritchard. Why didn't she simply divorce him?"

And then she knew Pritchard was lying. "She didn't believe in divorce," he said haughtily. "It wasn't an option Sheila was prepared to consider."

"Was she prepared to consider a contract killing, Mr Pritchard?"

'Grandpa Tony' looked furious. "You have absolutely no right . . . "

Mike moved in for the kill. "Someone paid to have Jonathan Selkirk murdered," he said venomously. "So far everything you've said here gives us more reason rather than less to believe it was his wife — or his son."

Pritchard looked startled. "I didn't come here to . . . "

Joanna studied the thin, handsome face with its hook nose. There was a superficial impression of strength, but Tony Pritchard had a weak chin and a narrow, mean-looking mouth with a twist of cruelty. It crossed her mind that Sheila Selkirk showed poor judgement when it came to men.

She leaned right across the desk so that her

face was inches away from his. "Selkirk was a wealthy man, wasn't he? Perhaps that was why she wasn't willing to consider divorce. After all, Mr Pritchard, a whole cake is twice as good as half a cake, isn't it?"

"That had nothing to do with it." Pritchard was full of righteous indignation. "He took up with a mistress . . . "

Joanna gave Mike a swift glance. This was not only news. It was at variance to Sheila Selkirk's comments on her husband's sexual prowess.

"Who was this mistress?" Her voice was casual but her fingers gripped the side of the desk.

"I'm not prepared to say."

"May I remind you, Mr Pritchard, that this is a murder investigation."

Mike chipped in, saying coolly, "It wouldn't happen to be the glamorous Miss Wilde, would it?"

Pritchard's shoulders twitched.

"Well, whoever it was, it turned out to be the last straw, didn't it, Mr Pritchard?" Mike had moved away from the door and was giving Pritchard one of his heavy looks. "He was a solicitor, and a clever one at that. He could have filched some money where it couldn't be traced and his wife would have been left with a lot less as a divorcee than as a merry widow. So her husband's death would have been worth a little — investment."

"Now look here . . . " Tony Pritchard began to bluster. "I came here this afternoon of my own volition, under my own steam. No one forced me to come."

Joanna lifted her plaster cast one inch from the desk. Her shoulder was aching. "And that's what puzzles us, Mr Pritchard. Why *did* you come?"

As she had expected, he had no answer ready.

* * *

"Now what was the point of all that?" Joanna asked as they watched him go.

"I don't know what the point was," Mike said grimly, "but it's had the effect of moving the suspicion straight to Selkirk's widow and son."

"You can't really believe Selkirk and Samantha Wilde were having an affair?"

Mike's frown was still directed at the door. "That was what he implied."

"Why? What was in it for her? It wasn't sex, was it?"

Mike shook his head.

"So it has to have been money." Joanna

stared around her. "But I can't see it somehow, can you? I mean, she's quite a . . . "

"Dollybird, while Jonathan Selkirk was . . . "

"An unattractive specimen. But then we've only Pritchard's word for it that they *were* having an affair."

Mike nodded.

Clumsily she draped her jacket round her shoulders. "Come on," she said, "we'd better follow up Pugh's offering and visit the hospital."

★ ★ ★

An ambulance was swinging out of the drive as they drove in. Through the black glass they could just make out a row of people squashed together. Joanna watched them with a sense of unease.

Mike noticed. "What's wrong?"

"I don't remember going in an ambulance," she said. "I can remember being on the side of the road and various other things. But I don't remember going in the ambulance."

"It'll come back." He pulled the car into a vacant slot and they approached the automatic doors.

The ward sister didn't look in the least bit pleased to see them. "I'd really like this

210

matter buried as soon as possible. It's bad publicity, and worrying for patients, relatives and staff." She gave Joanna a hard stare. "And when, Inspector, are we likely to get our fire door back?"

"I think it's best you get a new fire door fitted," Joanna said. "It's possible we might need to produce it in court as evidence. You can send the bill to the police department."

The nursing officer's face was hostile. "I don't suppose I have much choice in the matter, do I? Why have you come back?"

"We think . . . we think one of the nurses might have let the gunman in."

"Absolutely impossible," she said emphatically. "I trust my nurses absolutely. They are beyond suspicion."

"No one's beyond suspicion."

"Nurses have to be," she said.

"As in the Frost case?"

The nursing officer blinked. "That has nothing to do with Mr Selkirk's abduction," she said. "It was a tragic accident — a depressed, vulnerable man who was deeply unhappy." She stopped. "It's just coincidence . . . "

"That the same nurse was on duty both nights," Joanna said. "Two violent deaths taking place in the same, small hospital?" She watched the nursing officer carefully. "Would that be usual?"

"You know it wouldn't." They both knew she had been neatly caught.

"Is Yolande Prince back on duty?"

"No, but . . . " Her face froze. "Oh no," she said. "You can't think . . . " Her voice trailed away and the two police officers waited.

"She's still off sick. I haven't spoken to her," she said at last.

"And the other two?"

"Are back on days. They're on the wards now."

"Right, we'll talk to O'Sullivan first."

★ ★ ★

O'Sullivan sauntered in, his blue eyes sparkling with anticipated mischief-making.

"I thought you'd come back to me," he said. "You've taken your time about it." He sat down casually in the armchair, crossed his legs and leaned back. "But I suppose better late than never, eh?"

"Tell us a little more about the night Mr Selkirk disappeared," Joanna said. "Exactly what do you remember? Did you enter the room next to his? The one with the open window?"

O'Sullivan shook his head. "Now what would I be wantin' to go in that room for?"

he queried. "It was empty." He looked at them as though they were stupid. "There were no patients in there."

"And the door? Think for a moment before you answer."

"Shut," O'Sullivan said after pressing his fingertips to his temples in a theatrical gesture of thought. "Otherwise there would have been a draught. Doors bangin'."

She watched him carefully. "And what exactly did Selkirk say to you?"

O'Sullivan blinked. "He said that they wouldn't get him."

"You didn't mention this before. Who did he mean by 'they'?"

The nurse thought for a moment. "He said the family. Said he'd disappoint them yet. That he wasn't ready for his grave." He put his hands across the desk. "They all talk like that. Imagine their families are going to be havin' a fine time without them, spendin' all their hard-earned money."

Joanna leaned forward. "You imagined he was referring to his wife and son?"

"Well, who else would he be meanin'?"

Joanna gave Mike a quick glance, then turned back to the Irishman. "Now tell us about Frost. What exactly do you know about his death?" She met the blue eyes directly. "What did you actually *see*, O'Sullivan?"

"It was in the night," he said. "She'd been talkin' to him for ages before she went to give the drugs out — "

"You mean Yolande Prince," Joanna interrupted.

"Yes."

"Then what?"

"About an hour later I was workin' along the top end of the ward when I heard a sort of thump. I stuck my head out of the window and looked down into the car park. I could see a man lyin' there, in pyjamas. He was quite still. But she was screamin'. Like a mad thing she was, runnin' to the bathroom."

"What did you do?" Joanna spoke softly.

"I went runnin' to the bathroom too," O'Sullivan said. "As fast as I could."

Mike leaned closer and locked his eyes into O'Sullivan's. "You're a nurse," he said. "Why did you go there? Why didn't you ring for help or go down to the patient?"

O'Sullivan was leaning as far back in his chair as was possible without falling.

"Because," he said slowly, "I was wonderin' about her. What she was up to."

"But you didn't see him jump?"

O'Sullivan shook his head. "I was in the main ward," he said. "Frost must have jumped from the bathroom."

"Why?" said Mike.

"Because the bathroom windows are the only ones that open wide enough to let a person through. All the rest either have bars across or only open a few inches. It was a psychiatric ward."

"What did you expect to see in the bathroom?"

O'Sullivan's face grew meaner and thinner and there was gloating revenge in his eyes. "It was quite a climb to get out of that window."

The two detectives exchanged puzzled glances.

"You still don't understand, do you? In fact, no one did. No one ever did, except me. And I wasn't sayin'."

"Come on, O'Sullivan." Mike was losing patience with the game.

Joanna lifted her plastered arm and rested it on the desk. It was beginning to ache. "Did you tell all this to the inquiry?"

O'Sullivan gave her a shrewd glance. "I did." There was a short pause before he added, "It wasn't my fault if they didn't know what I meant."

"And what did you mean?"

"That man should have been on enough drugs to keep him asleep for hours," he said.

Joanna was just beginning to understand. "Go on," she said softly.

But O'Sullivan wasn't ready to tell all yet. "I thought she was goin' to follow him out the exact same way, until she saw me and stopped screamin.'"

"And when she saw you?"

"When she saw me she started to cry. She said she'd been counsellin' him." He gave a look of disgust. "I don't know who she thought she was — counsellin'. She'd had no trainin'."

"Get on with the story," Mike growled.

"He'd told her his life story," he said. "She'd listened and thought he was better and thought he didn't need his drugs. That's amateurs for you. And so Michael Frost — instead of being zonked out like a zombie — was awake enough to take a chair and climb out of the bathroom window. Because some stupid little nurse thought by listenin' she had made him better." He leaned closer. "I should have told the authorities there and then."

"Was she aware that you knew what had gone on?"

"Well . . . " O'Sullivan was enjoying himself. "I did comment he seemed very awake for a man on such sedation. It set her off screamin' again. Then I went to phone.

216

When I saw her a few minutes later she was returnin' the chair to its rightful place beside one of the beds. Tamperin' with evidence, I suppose you'd call it. Unless . . . "

Joanna was shocked. "You're surely not suggesting she assisted in the suicide?"

O'Sullivan's eyes darted from one to the other. "That's for you to decide."

"Did she give you any idea what they had been talking about?"

"Family trouble," O'Sullivan said casually. "She'd been tryin' to help him. But whatever she said to him made him worse because it wasn't very long after that he was doin' the highboard dive into the bloody car park."

Joanna winced. "Did Frost leave a suicide letter?"

O'Sullivan folded his arms. "Well, that's another thing," he said, obviously enjoying the attention. "At the inquest they said there was no note. But I distinctly saw her pocketing an envelope from the top of his locker."

"And you revealed none of this at the inquest?"

"Well, I wasn't goin' to spout my mouth and land myself in trouble."

"So this is the first anyone knows about it?"

O'Sullivan was unexpectedly silent and they guessed the rest.

"Apart from Yolande Prince," Joanna said sweetly. "Whom I suppose you threatened."

"Bloody cow." O'Sullivan was back to his usual insults. "Told me I couldn't prove a thing. But I could have made trouble. If I'd wanted to."

"How did Yolande seem on Monday night?"

"Lazy old bag," O'Sullivan said. "Skiving off all the rest of the week." He stared insolently at Joanna. "Do you know we haven't seen her since you found Selkirk's body all shot up?"

Soft little alarm bells began ringing in Joanna's head. But murder cases were like that. You saw corpses lurking behind every atypical statement.

"What was she like on Monday?"

"Forgetful," O'Sullivan said spitefully. "But then she always was a bit of a scatterbrain."

"Did she seem — on edge?" Joanna hated doing this, putting words into witnesses' mouths.

"Yes, come to think on it," he said, "she was — a bit."

"In what way?" Mike obviously did not believe this sudden surge of memory.

"Kept lookin' at her watch. As though she was waitin' for somethin' to happen."

"Did she have any phone calls that night?"

"No, but she jumped like a Mexican jumping bean every time the phone rang."

They glanced at each other, still sceptical.

"Do you know much about her private life?" Mike pressed.

O'Sullivan gave a loud expletive. "What bloody private life?"

"Just tell us what you do know, O'Sullivan."

"She lives in a little maisonette on the edge of the town. A tiny wee place with no room to swing a cat, but fairly near the hospital." He glowered at Mike. "She walks into work every day. Just a bit of a loner. I don't think she has that many friends." He stood up and laughed. "Just a budgerigar."

"Anything else you want to tell us?"

O'Sullivan shook his head and grinned. "I'd stay here talkin' all day long if it would get me out of takin' bedpans round to incontinent geriatrics. But I don't know any more." He leaned across the desk, his blue eyes flashing at Joanna. "I think you're wasting your time interviewing me. Looks like it's Yolande Prince is the one you should be talkin' to."

Joanna let the phone ring for five minutes before putting it down. The nursing officer met her eyes. "I didn't really think she would be there," she said. "Yolande is the sort of girl to go home to Mother when she's poorly."

"Where do her parents live?"

"Meir."

"I don't suppose you have their number?"

"Of course . . . "

This time the phone was picked up on the second ring and a woman's voice said hesitantly, "Hello?" She sounded elderly, a bit querulous.

"I'm ringing from the hospital," Joanna said "I wonder — is Yolande there, please?"

"She should be at work," her mother said happily. "She's just finished on nights. She's back on days now." She paused before asking curiously, "Who is this, please?"

That was when the alarm bells became deafening.

★ ★ ★

Mike chauffered Joanna the half-mile to Yolande's maisonette.

"I still fail to see what earthly connection

Frost's suicide could possibly have with Selkirk's murder," she exclaimed as they drew close.

Mike shot down a side road. "Maybe nothing," he said.

"I sincerely hope so," she replied with a sudden shiver, "or I wouldn't give tuppence for the life of Yolande Prince."

Mike pressed his foot hard down on the accelerator and screeched to a halt in front of a neat four-storeyed building.

The maisonette where Yolande lived was a small, purpose-built block, imaginatively set around a central grassy area which had been planted with miniature trees. There was a swing and a roundabout, but no children. Maybe they were all inside, watching TV or eating their tea or, more likely, both. Washing hung out across the balconies fluttered in the light breeze. They climbed the steps, passing clusters of milk bottles, and stopped outside a door with an accumulation of full bottles. Two had turned sour.

Mike battered the door with his ham fist. "She should be in," he said, "if she's sick."

"So why isn't she answering?"

They peered through the tiny window but could see little through the crack in the drawn curtains. Mike rapped on the window pane and waited. There was deathly silence.

They knew the flat was empty.

Joanna stood back. "We have to find her. She could be a key witness."

"Or a chief suspect," Mike said firmly.

She closed her eyes. Either was a more attractive prospect than . . .

Mike caught her panic. He hammered on the door again and bellowed through the letterbox.

Joanna touched his arm. "It's no good. The flat's empty. She isn't here."

Mike surveyed the door with resentment. Neither of them mentioned the bottles of milk.

"We're going to have to have a warrant, Joanna."

She nodded. "And Matthew's not going to be very pleased. We're supposed to be going out tonight. I think I'd better make a phone call."

★ ★ ★

Matthew's response was predictable.

"I'm sorry," she said. "The case is turning out to be a bit more sticky than I'd thought." She paused. "I have a bit of a problem. I'm not going to make it tonight."

She could picture his face, tight and set, no cleft in his chin, no dimples, eyes heavy green like dead moss. No sparkle, no warmth, just that contained, angry look.

"Well, I'm sorry too, actually, Joanna," he said bitterly.

"I'm really sorry. I'll see you when I see you."

The phone went dead.

"He's not too pleased." She made an attempt at a smile.

Mike didn't even look at her. "At some point, Joanna," he said, "you're going to have to make some pretty big decisions."

"I know," she said quietly. "I know."

★ ★ ★

Two uniformed officers joined them to break in to the flat. She could feel Mike's eyes on her long before he spoke.

"Have you got the same feeling as me?"

She nodded tensely. "Right here, in the pit of my stomach. Mike," she added, "why didn't we connect her sooner with Selkirk's abduction?"

He put a restraining hand on her arm as they watched the wood splinter. "Hold judgement, Jo. We don't know the facts yet."

It was a stout door, much harder to break down than the usual. In the end they had to use an axe. At last it gave way and they stepped into the dim hall, then through another door into the sitting room. The long curtains were still drawn.

Even in the dingy light they could see the shape of the nurse, slumped across the sofa. There was a faint scent of decay.

12

For a moment all four stood still. They'd been expecting this but it still came as a shock. Joanna broke the silence. She moved forward to touch the nurse's cheek. It was ice cold. "So," she said softly, "our killer had to step out from behind his cheque book. This time he's had to do his dirty work himself." She spoke into the two-way radio, rapping out the usual instructions with a horrid sense of déjà-vu.

"Get the SOCOs round here and the pathologist." She gave the address then turned back to the two officers. "The more we touch, the more evidence we risk destroying, so let's just look around the flat and leave the rest to the experts. You might just check the windows for signs of a forced entry."

It was again to Mike that she voiced her disturbing thoughts. "Maybe if we'd been sharper that night we interviewed her . . . "

He gave a brisk shake of his head. "Stop it, Jo. She's still in her uniform. At the time she was murdered we probably didn't even know Selkirk was dead. We couldn't have acted quicker."

But she knew it would continue to haunt her — this spectre. If only they'd realized that the fire door had been opened from the inside, then they would have kept a closer watch on the three nurses.

She gave a swift glance at the swollen, dark blue face and protruding tongue. How little people knew about their colleagues. The nursing officer had vouched for this girl and yet she must have been involved in Selkirk's abduction. And not just that. She must have led Gallini to Selkirk's bed, switched off the alarm on the heart machine, torn the electrode leads off and bundled him outside. For what? Money? What other motive could there have been? Money had certainly changed hands over Selkirk's murder. How natural, then, that a little more had had to be spent on the services of a nurse because of his hospitalization.

Because of the letter.

And as she wandered around the flat Joanna had a feeling of abject failure. She knew most of the facts and yet she still knew little of the mechanics for Selkirk and Yolande's murders. She had met and assessed Yolande Prince and not suspected any involvement in Selkirk's disappearance.

She forced herself to gaze again, not on the face this time but on the nurse's dark uniform, now in disarray, the thick stockings, the clumpy shoes. *Why?* That was the question that screamed in her mind. If she had been on her own in the flat with no colleagues she would have screamed it out loud. *Why?* And why was Michael Frost the only reply she could think of?

The two police constables wandered back into the sitting room. "Even the bloody budgie's dead," the young PC said gloomily. "Must have starved."

Mike's eyes were trained on Joanna. She stared back at him and knew he would be echoing the very same question.

"Why did she get involved?"

He shrugged. "Who knows?"

The wait for the SOCOs and the pathologist always seemed endless. They could do nothing except fill the time with a second, superficial search. There was no answer to their question, few personal letters or photographs. The flat told them little.

Yolande had been a tidy girl of modest means. Her home held no luxuries. Her clothes were chainstore, her perfumes middle market and inexpensive. The same was true of make-up and the contents of her kitchen. And the decorations were neat and unimaginative. There was no hint of avarice.

"She didn't do it for money."

Mike frowned. "Why else?"

"Just a thought," she said slowly, apologetically.

"If not for money, what about a moral reason?"

"You mean Rowena Carter?"

She nodded.

He gave a wry laugh. "I suppose she would have heard about the case. You think she saw herself as an avenging angel?"

She watched his face change as he thought about it.

"Could be."

"You realize, then, that she must have had some contact with the person who organized Selkirk's murder?"

"Seems like it," he said cautiously.

"And they must have persuaded her to help in the abduction of Selkirk. So was it was someone Yolande already knew?"

She paused to think. "They must have been very persuasive to have conned her into helping."

"Unless they had some hold over her . . . "

"Over the Michael Frost case. So here we are, Mike." Her eyes were sharp. "We've come full circle. And so this blameless girl, home-loving and indulged by her parents, praised by her employers, somehow got herself involved in — of all things — a contract killing."

Even as she spoke she was shaking her head. "At the very least, I'm surprised, in fact I'm bordering on the sceptical." Her eyes wandered back to the dead girl. "She had me fooled."

Mike was silent and she aired her thoughts out loud. "What did O'Sullivan say? She'd been talking to Frost for an hour before he jumped." She met Mike's eyes. "I wonder what he said."

"We'll never know now, Jo."

"I'm banking on us finding out, Korpanski."

Mike was scratching his chin with the tip of his thumb. It was a habit he had when struggling to think. The rasping sound was threatening to annoy her. He stopped doing it just in time and looked up. "She couldn't have known Selkirk was going to be murdered," he said, "or she wouldn't have had anything to do with it. If you remember, Jo, when we spoke to her she seemed confident he'd turn up, didn't she? What if she thought he was just going to be abducted — or kidnapped for money — or something," he finished lamely.

She nodded. "Maybe."

One of the uniformed officers returned from a tour of the building's exterior.

"No sign of a break-in," he said. "My guess is that she let the killer in herself."

Joanna forced herself to bend over the girl's body and study the neck. Twined around it, lying loosely now, was a nylon stocking.

"Let's go outside," she said suddenly.

It was dusk. The lights of the town looked falsely welcoming. One of them shone on a murderer. Distant traffic roared along the road. No sign yet of flashing blue lights.

"It's time to go right back to the beginning, Mike," she said decisively. "I think we'd better speak to the Selkirks again, both mother and son and not forgetting Grandpa Tony." She stopped and gritted her teeth. "In fact, in the mood I'm in I could even suspect pretty little Lucy or our pregnant mare."

Mike looked at her in surprise.

"And then," she said, "I'm going to revisit the Carter family."

She couldn't ignore Mike any longer. "All right, all right. They lost their daughter. I'm sorry for them. I really am, but someone had Selkirk killed and that led to this."

"Joanna," he objected, "they wouldn't have killed Yolande."

"Not even to get at Selkirk?"

He shook his head. "Not after three years."

And the infuriating thing was, she knew he was right. She couldn't see either of the

Carters having any involvement in the nurse's death. Their hatred had all been centred on the man who had destroyed . . . no, murdered . . . their daughter. But it hadn't made them lose their humanity. They would not have killed Yolande Prince.

Perhaps it was the enforced inactivity of the wait for Matthew and the SOCOs, or the return to the small room, but now a new horror was beginning to take shape. "Surely," she said, "surely, Michael Frost's death *was* suicide?"

Mike, as usual, was prosaic. "Well, pushing someone out of a window would be a clumsy method of murder."

She agreed.

"Maybe the point isn't so much *whether* he committed suicide as why?"

"Why what?" she said irritably.

"Why did he commit suicide?"

She frowned. "Because he was depressed."

"Yeah, but why was he depressed?"

She stared at him. "I don't know."

"Don't they usually have a reason? Maybe there's something there."

She stared at him. "We could certainly follow it up," she said, "see if anyone knows."

"She must have known," he said. "She was the one who was talking to him just before he jumped. I bet he told her everything. She knew why he was depressed. She must have done. Maybe that's why she did what she did. I know I'm right, Jo," he added defensively.

"And it cost her her life?"

Mike was standing behind her. "She didn't put up much of a struggle, did she?" He glanced around the room. "No broken furniture. She just sat there and let whoever it was walk behind her and do it."

★ ★ ★

The SOC officers, when they finally arrived, were a pleasure to watch, she thought as they began working methodically around the room, starting with the door, moving along the hall carpet, examining the walls for stains, brushing surfaces with fingerprint dust, taking sellotape samples from the long curtains.

With them worked the police photographer, who snapped every conceivable angle and drew diagrams to illustrate, hopefully in court, the positions of everything in the room.

Outside the front door a small cluster of neighbours was gathering. Joanna detailed the two uniformed officers to start gathering statements. "I'll talk to anyone later who thinks they saw something."

They nodded and disappeared outside.

It was another half an hour before Matthew arrived. And, like waiting for an ambulance, the time seemed long and impossibly drawn out. She heard his car pull up outside, the steps taken two at a time, then the door being pushed open. Timberland shoes, jeans, a navy sweater, the familiar honey-coloured tousled hair and a more familiar expression. He was smiling.

"Well, good thing you cancelled," he said ruefully.

She nodded and made a face. "Look," she awkwardly, trying to keep her voice low. She was aware of the room full of watching police officers. "I know we need to talk but it'll have to wait until this case is finished. We're all working flat out, Matthew. I'm sorry."

He gave her a quick look which carried in it an accusation that she didn't care enough. "I don't know whether you've noticed, Joanna, but our relationship," he said very quietly, "is permanently on a back burner. I think I warrant more than that."

She stood miserably, at a loss, and was relieved to hear Sergeant Barraclough clearing his throat behind her.

She put her hand on Matthew's arm.

"A weekend away," she said urgently. "I promise, somewhere luxurious. As soon as this case is sorted. Please, Matthew."

He stared at her for a moment, then turned away and directed his attention to the victim. There was an immediate change in his manner, an absorption in the thin face as he snapped on a pair of surgeon's gloves and opened his black Gladstone bag.

"Nasty business," he said as he fingered the stocking draped around the neck, prised open the glazed eyes. "Petechiae," he murmured. He examined her tongue. He worked so swiftly and deftly, as she had seen so many times before.

It was only ten minutes later that he straightened up. "Superficially," he said, "I'd say she's been dead three or four days. "Putrefaction." He gave an apologetic laugh. "Sorry." He held up his hands. "I know you hate it. Ten guesses as to the cause of death." He touched the stocking. "Easy, really. Strong stuff — pulled hard. Not even knotted. Just pulled very tight." He stopped. "Crossed over at the back. Shock and strong hands," he said.

"How strong?" she asked. "Can women be excluded?"

He shook his head. "Unfortunately not. The element of surprise, plus a quick flick of the wrist." He tapped her plaster cast. "You couldn't have done it though, Jo."

"Thanks," she said drily. "That really narrows the field."

He was peeling off his disposable gloves. "I suppose she's connected with the Selkirk case?"

Joanna nodded. "She was on duty at the hospital that night. She was probably the one who let the murderer into the hospital."

Matthew raised his eyebrows. "It's the same . . . ?"

"Not in a month of Sundays," she said. "Not his style."

"So who . . . ?"

"You tell me."

"When was she last seen alive?"

"The morning Selkirk was missed." She stopped. "I interviewed her."

"I think she died within a few hours of speaking to you." He turned his head round. "Didn't they miss her at the hospital?"

"Someone rang her in sick, claiming to be her mother. The story fitted so well, that she'd had such a shock the doctor had said she should have some time off to recover. No one suspected a thing."

"Well, it looks as though she was murdered soon after getting home." He gave the ghost of a smile. "She's still in uniform."

She met the light in his eyes. "We had noticed."

"Sorry." He raised his hand in mock defence. "Not trying to tell you your job."

"Good."

"I'll get in touch with the Coroner," he said, "and provisionally we'll set the PM for nine tomorrow morning. OK with you?"

She nodded.

"You're giving me a lot of work lately." He grinned at her affectionately.

"Unfortunately." She looked down at the body. "I wish *this* hadn't happened. She was a decent girl."

Joanna stared out of the first-floor window across the town. Even by night she could pick out landmarks. Pinnacles of churches, the late-night supermarket and beyond that the deep, empty black of the Staffordshire moorlands. She sighed.

Something pricked at her consciousness and she wandered into the kitchen to find Korpanski.

"The morning before Selkirk's death," she said slowly, "he got a letter, didn't he?"

Mike nodded.

"We thought it was meant to frighten him and it did, enough to give him a heart attack."

Mike demurred.

"I know. I know. I'm not saying the person who hired Gallini anticipated that, but it did, and he'd had letters before, hadn't he?" She was using him as a sounding-board. "The others had been sent by the Carter family."

Mike nodded in agreement, wondering where all this was leading.

But Joanna was not to be hurried. "And they'd rattled him enough for him to contact the police. We warned them off. This new letter upset him again but this time he didn't consult the police but asked his partner to deal with it, or so Wilde claims."

"Wilde had already drafted out a reply."

"Incriminating evidence if the subject of the telephone conversation was not the letter but something else."

Mike sighed. "We can't ever prove what they talked about."

"And that's the problem of a murder investigation. You never know who's lying and who's telling the truth. And sometimes people hide things for no good reason."

"So where does that lead us?"

Joanna gave a quick laugh. "I don't know, Mike. I'm simply bouncing ideas off you."

"Back to the letter," Mike said. "The Carters deny sending it."

"As someone once said, they would, wouldn't they?"

"Then where does that leave us as far as the letter is concerned?"

"It's clouded the entire issue."

"Either that or it's the sternest pointer towards the truth, but I'm certain that no one could possibly have known that Selkirk would be so intimidated by the letter that he would be admitted to hospital. No one," she said emphatically. "Not his wife. Not his doctor." She paused. "And certainly not Gallini himself. But he *was* admitted and that must have meant a sudden change of plan. Someone must have instructed Gallini where to find Selkirk and just as suddenly they had to rope someone in to make sure Gallini got Selkirk out of the hospital without discovery."

She motioned towards the living room door. "It was poor old Yolande's bad luck that she was the one they picked on, which leads us to wonder why. Why her? What hold did they have over her? What lever could they have used to coerce her into something so against her nature? And again, Mike, we're back to the Frost case, which seems the only blemish on an otherwise unexceptional and exemplary life."

She peered out of the window through the slats of the blind. "Now if the connection had been with poor little Rowena Carter's accident I could have understood the whole thing better, but a suicide . . . " She drew in a deep breath. "Once we've spoken to Yolande's parents we'd better study the facts surrounding Michael Frost's suicide a bit closer. OK?"

They moved back to the sitting room and Joanna took a last look at Yolande. She turned back to Mike. "Let's get her out of here," she said. "Let the SOCOs have their way. Call a briefing for 8 p.m. and get all the files on the Frost case out. And get on to forensics for the comparison of the letter Selkirk got the morning he died with the Carter ones, will you?"

* * *

It was a half-hour journey to Meir, to a small, neat box of a house with a tidy, manicured front garden.

The lights were on, the curtains undrawn. They were being watched.

The front door opened as they walked up the path and a little black Scottie dog snapped at their heels.

An elderly couple were framed in the doorway, the man with his arm protectively around the woman's shoulders. They made no attempt to call off the dog.

Joanna flashed her ID card. "Detective Inspector Piercy. And this is Detective Sergeant Korpanski, she said gently. "We're from the Leek Police. May we come in? I'm afraid we have some bad news."

She recognized them from one of the photographs she'd seen in the maisonette. The father was elderly with a bent back and a military-style moustache, the woman plump and wearing an apron. She was fumbling with the strings, then finally tugged hard enough to snap them. She whisked it off over her head.

They sat in the dining room, formally gathered around a cheap teak table with a white ring in the centre where a vase must have stood. Joanna cleared her throat.

"What's happened?" It was the man who spoke. "After you rang we tried to telephone her." He looked confused. "There was no answer. And at work they said she'd been off all week." He asked the same question again. "What's happened? Is she all right?"

"I'm afraid we found her dead in her flat," Joanna said gently. She had learned to break bad news by degree. Let them know she was dead first. Give them time to digest that unpalatable fact before telling them the rest.

The man was of a stern constitution.

"Dead," he said bluntly. "How?"

"We're not absolutely sure yet," Joanna said cautiously. "There'll have to be a — "

"Post-mortem?" the man said brutally.

Joanna nodded.

"Well, how do you think she died?" His eyes were grey and watering. "Not natural causes. She was a healthy girl."

Joanna took a deep breath. "We have reason to believe someone may have got into her flat. It looks as though she was strangled." She paused. "I'm so sorry."

The woman dissolved then. "She's a gentle girl, our Yolande," she said. "All we've got, you know." She sniffed loudly. "We've only got the one."

She would learn to change the tense.

"She's so gentle and kind too. Always helping people. Always helping people."

The man was gripping the arms of his chair. His knuckles showed bone-white. "Was it one of them sex maniacs?"

"We can't be sure," Joanna said. "Not until we have the results of the post-mortem. But no, I don't think so. We think it happened some time last Tuesday."

The woman looked appalled. "And she's been lying there all this time? On her own?"

Joanna nodded.

"Our girl — my daughter — lying dead — untended?"

The man stared at Joanna. "Who did it," he said, and then, "what can we do to help get him?"

"We're going to want to take a statement — later."

"Now!" the man almost shouted. "Ask your questions now."

"We don't usually in cases — "

His eyes were bulging. "*Ask them*," he said through gritted teeth.

"We think," Joanna said gently, "that Yolande's death was somehow connected with other incidents at the hospital."

"That solicitor chap?"

"Possibly. Did she say anything about it?"

Yolande's father nodded. "She rang us after you'd been questioning her. She sounded fine. Said he'd be turning up none the worse for his experience." He was moving his head backwards and forwards. "She was sure nothing would happen to him. It gave us a shock when you found him dead."

Both Mike and Joanna were silent for a moment, digesting this piece of information, then Joanna leaned across the table. "What can you tell us about Michael Frost?"

Mr Prince looked puzzled. It was not what

he had expected. "Michael Frost," he said slowly. "Was that the man who jumped out of the window? That was ages ago. What on earth has he got to do with this?" He crumpled in the chair.

His wife put her hand on his arm. "I remember about Michael Frost," she said quietly.

Joanna turned to her. "What did Yolande say about him?"

"He was only a young man," she said. "His wife had been ill. He was depressed about it. Yolande spoke to him. She tried to comfort him a bit. It was awful for her. She thought she'd cheered him up a bit. He said he felt better. So she thought he was all right again." She stopped. "He said he didn't need his tablets that night. He'd made some tough decision and he felt better, much better. She didn't bother watching him after that. She saw him writing something. The next thing she knew he'd gone through the window. She couldn't believe it. And there was this letter, you see, addressed to his wife. She put it in her pocket. She was so frightened." The woman's eyes were abstract and bleak. "Then once she'd hidden the letter there was nothing she could do. She couldn't just produce it in court. But it did explain everything."

"What did it say?"

"She didn't tell me," Mrs Prince said proudly. "She was a loyal girl, loyal to her patients. Always kept their secrets for them. But it would have made things easier for her, especially when that O'Sullivan man started making such trouble. Making snide remarks."

Both the detectives could well imagine that.

Mrs Prince looked at each of them carefully. "She did feel responsible, you see. She'd been sitting talking to him. We went to the inquest," she said. "They didn't blame her, you know. Everyone said — even the Coroner — that she'd done all she could. It was the hospital inquiry that asked why she'd been on a psychiatric ward in the first place. Yolande was off sick for a long time afterwards. She felt so responsible. She only wanted to help him. She thought she had. She was one of these girls with a strong social conscience," she said. She pressed her hand across her mouth. "She was our only child. What have we got left now?"

13

The mortuary was hardly Joanna's favourite place to be at nine o'clock on a Saturday morning, but she would not be alone. As Mike dropped her off she saw the cars of the SOCO team waiting in the car park, as well as Matthew's BMW.

An officer she knew, Barraclough, greeted her with a wave. "Dr Levin's already inside."

Matthew was gowned up, impatient to start. He barely greeted her before he focused his attention on the body.

All post-mortems begin in the same way. The body must be naked. So first of all Yolande's uniform had to be cut off and the stocking removed from around her neck. The same care was given to her overwashed, faded underclothes, but it was when Matthew began to examine her neck that he took particular interest. Even Joanna could see the extensive bruising where the stocking had been pulled tight. Beneath the skin the tiny hyoid bone had been broken.

Half an hour later she was drinking coffee in Matthew's office. "Pretty obvious, really," he said. "She was strangled. She did try to fight off her attacker. There are marks on her fingers and a couple of broken nails from where she tried to pull away the stocking but she didn't have much of a chance. From the evidence it was quick and unexpected. And the person who killed her was strong as well as having the distinct advantage of surprise. After all," he pointed out grimly, "Yolande was a fit, healthy girl. Not so easy to kill."

"Was it a man?"

Matthew sighed. "A man or a strong woman." There was a glint of humour in his eyes. "I do wish you wouldn't make such a concerted effort to get me to name the murderer."

She held up her hand. "Sorry."

"All I can give you is a cause of death — strangulation."

Barraclough took her back to the station and she found Mike waiting for her.

"Did you get Justin Selkirk's address?"

He nodded, failing to hide an involuntary smirk. "Lou-lou gave it to me," he said, "after a bit of a struggle. She's very hot on human rights as well as being protective towards her employee. I think she's hiding something."

Joanna laughed. "You think everyone's hiding something, Mike."

"No," he said earnestly. "I mean it. She

really didn't want me talking to him again."

"Well, tough," Joanna said, "because he's next on my list. So where does he live?"

"You're not going to believe this."

★ ★ ★

They parked the squad car at the entrance to the field where a dirt track led to the caravan. On a bright summer's day it might have looked idyllic, a great, gypsy adventure, but today, in a fine grey drizzle, it looked bleak.

Yet this was where Justin Selkirk lived.

Joanna stared at it incredulously. "Are you sure they live here, Mike?"

"This is where she said. I did check."

"But the family are worth thousands. That great big house and Jonathan Selkirk allowed his son, daughter-in-law and granddaughter to live here?"

Mike read the entry from his notebook. "The caravan standing near the entrance to Dallow's Farm." He pushed the gate open. "Besides which, isn't that his car?"

Parked next to the caravan was the distinctive yellow and rust Citroën 2CV.

"Pritchard didn't really need to come down and tell us what a sod Selkirk was," he observed. "We only had to come and visit his son. He must have hated his father."

"Or do you mean the father must have hated the son?" They walked on a few paces before Joanna thought further. "You know, I don't think hate's the word. Selkirk wanted to belittle his son, make him feel inadequate. It probably suited him that he was reduced to living like this — such an obvious failure."

"No wonder Selkirk ended up with a hole in his head."

"Ssh," Joanna said, and raised her hand to knock at the caravan door.

Teresa Selkirk must have heard their voices. She tugged it open before the first knock. Her pale face looked only mildly surprised as she recognized them. "Oh, it's you. Hello." She gave one of her vague smiles and pulled the door behind her. "It isn't terribly convenient at the moment. We're rather busy."

"We won't keep you long, Mrs Selkirk. We really wanted to talk to your husband."

"Justin?" Her narrow eyebrows arched. "You want to speak to Justin? What about?"

"Well, it was his father who was shot," Mike said brusquely, "and we're still investigating."

"I thought you'd arrested the man." She waved her hands around. "The papers said you had."

"Someone hired him, Mrs Selkirk. We thought your husband might be able to help us with our enquiries."

An expression of sharp intelligence crossed Teresa's face. "Is that a euphemism for arresting him, Inspector?"

"No, Mrs Selkirk, it isn't. If we were going to arrest him we would have said so. We merely want to talk to him. Is he in?"

Teresa Selkirk's face changed to one of mild amusement. She flattened herself against the door. "He is. In the drawing room, actually."

She hadn't lied when she'd claimed they were busy. It was a small living area and the floor was cluttered with bundles of clothes tied up with string. Justin was sitting in the corner on a grubby orange foam seat. His daughter was on his knee, drawing on his outstretched palm with an extended index finger. As they watched she clapped her hands then looked up. Round, baby eyes watched warily. Teresa sank down on a heap of blankets, one hand holding her back, the other resting on her stomach.

"Twinges," she explained. "I keep getting them."

"Why have you come here?" Justin asked in his high-pitched voice. "I can't help you. I thought you realized that. I hardly saw my father. I don't know anything about his murder."

"We understand that you and your father didn't get along too well."

"I would have done. He didn't want to be bothered with me. Tell them, Teresa."

"How long have you lived here?"

"About eight months. We fell behind with the mortgage. Things were difficult. It wasn't my fault." Justin's face trembled. "We tried to manage. But with Lucy and another baby on the way it was hard. The more we got behind the more they pestered us, didn't they?"

His wife nodded.

"And our house had dropped in value. The only way out was to sell and try to pay off the debt." Justin reached across and squeezed his wife's hand. "The farmer said we could live here until we got sorted out. It's got a drain, mains water and electricity. We've managed," his face dropped, "in a way."

"Couldn't you have moved into your parents' house?"

"Justin's father wouldn't have allowed it," Teresa said coldly. "He believed couples of our age had responsibilities. He was very anxious we stand on our own two feet, as he liked to put it."

"You did ask, then?"

Teresa bent her head and her black hair dropped like a curtain. It was impossible to read her expression. "We did."

Mike was incredulous. "He wouldn't put you up, even for a short time?"

Teresa Selkirk lifted her head and gave another calm smile. "You didn't know my father-in-law," she said. "Anyway, sometimes things happen for the best. We're getting out of here now. Aren't we, Justin?"

Her husband gave her a swift, grateful glance and buried his face in the child's curls.

"Where are you moving to?"

"We're moving in with my mother-in-law."

"How very convenient."

For the first time Teresa Selkirk took a good look at Mike. "What would you know about it?" she said, gently, not unpleasantly. She was goading him.

Mike flushed.

She pursued him. "Ever lived in a tiny little caravan like this with your wife and child? Or have you got a proper home? And it'll only be a couple of weeks before there's four of us here. You want to try it some time, Sergeant. My mother-in-law, bless her, would have given us a home any time. It was only that old sod who stopped her. Justin has had a very difficult life."

They turned to look at Justin Selkirk, still apparently absorbed in his daughter. The child was teasing them, giggling and peeping through her fingers. Her father was watching with a wary, absorbed expression on his thin, pale face.

Perhaps it was then that Joanna realized there was something different about Justin Selkirk.

He glanced up then shyly, met her eyes, and gave a slow, deliberate wink. Was he a clever fool or a foolish fool? She watched him play with the child's curls, long, strong, bony fingers wrapping the yellow hair tightly. Then, quite suddenly, and without warning, he pulled. The child yelled. Pain flashed across her face before she laughed again, with tears shining in her eyes.

Teresa watched without emotion. "Don't do that, Justin," she warned. "Please, don't do that."

Immediately Justin Selkirk stopped playing with the child's hair and dropped his hands to his sides. The child almost toppled before grabbing on to his sweater.

His wife's face sagged. She looked older, bleaker, and frightened. This much both the police officers read before she again bowed her head and used the curtain of hair to conceal her emotions.

Joanna felt compelled to divert the conversation back to Selkirk's murder. "Your father's death must have upset you very much, Mr Selkirk."

"Yes, it did. It was an absolutely awful shock." The glimpse they had had of Justin Selkirk had been replaced by Selkirk the ham actor with predictably awful lines. "I don't think I shall ever get over it." He met their eyes with an expression of fatal grief. "We shall never forget him."

"A terrible shock," Joanna said softly but Teresa Selkirk picked her head up and gave her a penetrating stare.

"Haven't you two understood anything?"

There was a long silence.

Selkirk broke it. "Do you know," he said, "I have dreams about my father's murder. I actually dreamed about it the night he disappeared."

"Really, Mr Selkirk?" Mike could hardly contain his interest.

"Even now . . . " Selkirk glanced around him fearfully, "I think I hear his voice."

"And what does he say?"

Selkirk closed his eyes. "He screams."

★ ★ ★

It was Mike who spoke first as they paddled back through the mud. "It looks as though Selkirk handed on a bit of his character to his son."

Joanna nodded.

"I know it's just imagination," he continued, "but I've met mass murderers I've been more comfortable with than that little trio."

★ ★ ★

The officers were unusually attentive during the Saturday briefing.

Yolande's murder had heightened the feeling of pressure. All felt a certain sense of failure — of anti-climax, of disappointment. They knew the person morally responsible for both murders was still walking free. Each gave their findings dully in voices taut with stress. Sure, in their dreams it might be an arrest followed by a conviction, but their worst nightmares gave them something quite different from fear — another investigation scaled down because of the cost and pressure of other cases. The police force was not financed by an elastic budget. Joanna watched them file out quietly. Cases were always like this. The first couple of briefings ended boisterously, with confident jokes, the inevitable leg-pulling. But this acceptance, these bowed shoulders. The officers could not work overtime for ever. After one week they were getting tired and their families would soon be complaining, adding to the pressure.

She turned to Mike after the last one had left.

"You get yourself to the gym. Take a bit of time off."

He was quick to demur but she touched his shoulder. It didn't suit her plans to have Mike at her elbow all evening.

"I mean it, Mike," she said. "Work off a bit of that energy. I want to run some routine checks on the Frost case."

The file on Michael Frost was quite thin. There had been very little formal police investigation and no reason to suspect that his death was anything but a psychiatric suicide. His depression was well documented. The consultant psychiatrist had spoken of the patient's anguish and grief following years of nursing his wife through a long illness.

Yes, the suicide had been both unexpected and tragic. Yes, on reflection he should have been on a ward with closer supervision.

Joanna gave a wry smile as she read the transcript of the consultant's statement. It was very difficult to prevent a really determined suicide bid, she read. Very difficult. The future of depressives was assured, she read. The psychiatric ward was now situated on the first floor, staffed with trained mental nurses. The windows had all been barred. There were double the number of staff on duty at any one time. No untrained nurse was to be left in sole charge.

Joanna threw the file down on the desk. It all sounded too good to be true. Where was this all leading her?

She picked it up again and glanced through the pathologist's report. Frost had suffered horrendous injuries. Head, chest, pelvis. Two broken legs.

Yolande would have heard all this evidence. How must she have felt?

Another sentence jumped out at her. No one had assessed him a suicide risk.

She looked again through the post-mortem report. There was no record of the toxicology analysis. So if O'Sullivan was right and Yolande Prince had not given Frost his medication, they were the only two who knew ... unless the letter had revealed more. She was suddenly curious about that letter. To whom had it been addressed? To the invalid wife?

Had Yolande pocketed it, then passed it on without revealing its existence?

The last sheet of paper in the file was the

published results of the hospital inquiry. And it was this that had been more damning of Yolande Prince.

She had stepped outside her bounds of duty trying to advise the patient.

She should have realized the desperate state of her patient and called for medical aid.

She should have consulted the night sister.

She should have made sure the bathroom window was locked and secured. No mention of a chair.

In all there were fourteen criticisms aimed at the nurse and Joanna felt a wash of sympathy for her.

They had used her as a scapegoat for the tragic death of a patient. Joanna could well see it would have made Yolande Prince both notorious and vulnerable. The local paper had hounded her for weeks before forgetting the case.

Forgetting? Joanna admonished herself. The press never forgot.

★ ★ ★

She rang Matthew at his flat. "Matthew," she said, "tell me about depression. Does it have to have a cause?"

He gave an explosive laugh. "I don't know,

257

Joanna. You cancel our night out and then the next day instead of apologizing or, even better, arranging another seductive evening, you ask me about depression?"

"I do it because I love you," she said, "because I can depend on you and because I know you know the answer."

"Hmm. Well," he said slowly, "thinking on depression has changed recently. I believe the current theory is that it does need a cause. At least . . . " The logical scientist won over the doctor, the love of precision, "not really a cause so much as a reason. It's usually there, although frequently the relatives fail to recognize the severity of the resulting depression. That's the trouble. Depressed people's small problems tend to increase in size. The depression makes them magnify their problems thus increasing the severity of the initial depression."

"And will someone who commits suicide usually have tried before?"

"Not necessarily."

"I see."

"What's depression got to do with your case?"

"Plenty," she said. "At least I think so."

"And how are you getting on with it?"

"I think I'm just starting to understand," she said slowly.

"Do you want picking up and taking home?"

"No. Thanks," she said awkwardly. "It's really nice of you but I'll cadge a lift home. I've got some more work I want to catch up on, plus an early start in the morning."

"Don't overdo it."

She felt suddenly touched by his concern. She pictured the strength in his face that could so suddenly turn warm and gentle. She fell silent and Matthew, with his intuitive understanding of her moods, said nothing until he tentatively broached the subject of the weekend. "You haven't forgotten about our little romantic break for two, have you?"

"No," she said. "Definitely not."

His voice was even softer when he asked the next question. "And you will consider the future?"

"I promise."

"Good." He sounded satisfied. "I'll see you soon, then?"

"Yes."

* * *

Luckily for Joanna WPC Critchlow was on duty and available for the rest of the evening. Joanna found her chatting to the

259

duty sergeant by the coffee machine.

"I hate to be sexist about this," she said. Dawn turned a pair of enquiring dark eyes on her. "I need someone to come with me."

"And Korpanski won't do?"

Joanna shook her head. "I need the kid gloves of the female of the species."

"I'm intrigued." Dawn unhooked a set of car keys from behind the desk. "Where to?"

"Emily Place, number fourteen."

★ ★ ★

It was strange, Joanna reflected during the ten-minute drive, how much people's style of driving differed. Mike was heavy on the accelerator and bad language. Dawn Critchlow made the car positively glide.

Emily Place was deserted, the residents' curtains tightly drawn against a dull, cold evening. There was nothing to tempt people out of doors when inside there was the fire, warmth, light, the television. They could hear the Carters' TV on loud as they walked up the concrete path, threading themselves past a rusting car.

"Tidy-looking place," Dawn observed. "Do you want me to come in or shall I wait outside?"

"Come with me," Joanna said. "I want

260

you to hear all that's said."

Andy Carter opened the door to her knock. He gave them both a hostile stare.

"I don't believe this," he said. "You've been here once. We've told you everything. I was hoping you wouldn't come back." His Adam's apple bobbed around in his thin neck. "I suppose I was being a bit optimistic, wasn't I?" He stood back while they entered.

Ann Carter was lying on the sofa, watching television. She hardly looked up as the two officers walked in. "And I don't suppose you've brought any good news for us, have you?"

Dawn perched on a dining chair with thin, spider legs.

Joanna sank down on the sofa beyond Ann's feet. "And what would you consider good news, Mrs Carter?"

The woman merely stared back at her. She opened dry lips. No words came out.

Andy Carter took a seat beside his wife. They watched Joanna warily.

Joanna felt the domination of the photographs lining the walls of this small room. For a moment she stared at the largest of them.

"She was a sweet little girl, wasn't she?"

Andy Carter raised his eyes heavenwards.

"Yes," he said through clenched teeth. "She was."

Joanna's eyes were drawn to the missing photograph. The Carters saw her look. They must have read her puzzlement. They exchanged glances but said nothing.

"You must miss her."

Andy Carter's hand jerked in his wife's. "What do you think?" he asked furiously. "What do you bloody think? Oh!" he exclaimed impatiently. "Is any of this going to bring her back?"

"No. But then Selkirk's death wasn't going to resurrect your daughter, was it?" Joanna let her gaze linger over the photograph.

"We didn't have anything to do with his death," Carter spoke angrily. His face was a dark, angry red and she knew the pushing was having effect. He stood up, agitated. "What's the bloody point of all this? Can't you see? We're still raw from our daughter's death."

"I've come from another house today," Joanna said quietly. "They'd lost an only daughter too."

"Send them Victim Support, then," Ann Carter snapped. Her face was contorted with grief. "That's what you did for us. Big help they were too."

Joanna waited for the outburst to finish

before carrying on. "You might know the girl."

Neither looked curious.

"She was a nurse."

"Oh, yeah?" Andy Carter pulled at the gold sleeper in his ear. "Not five years old, then, like our Row."

"No, but every bit as precious to her parents."

He flushed. "They have my sympathy," he mumbled.

But Ann Carter's face was still hard. "What are you doing round here, Inspector?" she sneered." Come to admire our photographs?"

Joanna paused. The television in the corner of the room continued to spew out colour and sound. She wished they would switch it off. Somehow they seemed able to ignore it. She couldn't.

"The girl's name was Yolande," she said, "Yolande Prince. She worked at the cottage hospital."

Andy Carter let out a whistle of breath. "That's where I've heard that name," he said. "I knew I'd read it somewhere." He gave Joanna a penetrating stare. "She was the nurse on duty the night Selkirk disappeared, wasn't she?"

Joanna nodded.

They were both watching her now, their

interest at last pricked.

Joanna leaned closer. "Who's Michael Frost?" she asked abruptly.

Ann Carter swung her feet to the floor, stood up, crossed the room and turned the television off. The room was abruptly empty, devoid of light, colour, noise. It seemed suddenly both plain and dull.

The woman picked one of the photographs from the wall and stared at it for a while without speaking. "When Selkirk crashed into the crossing outside the school he killed our Rowena. Molly Frost was the lollipop lady. She lost both her legs. Michael was her husband. He took it bad."

The simple words were an obvious understatement.

At last. Joanna felt an enormous sense of relief wash over her as she listened to Ann Carter.

"Michael was wonderful," she said. "He gave up his job to look after Molly. Cared for her like she was a baby." She gave Joanna a twisted smile. "Although Rowena died we never blamed Molly. We knew she had done her best. She would have saved her if she could have. She did try. We always felt grateful."

Her husband put his arm around her, gave her a kiss on her cheek. Then he wiped the corner of his eye and sat down again.

"It was too much for Michael." He took up the story. "Watching over Molly all day every day, and her in such pain." He stopped. "Her spine were damaged. She were never free of it. The week before Michael had to go in with his depression there were talk of Molly having to go to one of them hospices and have proper care. He felt such a failure. The pair of them." He gave a frustrated laugh. "He felt he'd failed Molly and Molly felt she'd failed Rowena." Some of his anger surfaced. "And really it was that bastard Selkirk who should have taken the blame for it all, but he didn't care. He got off scot free. No driving ban or anything. I saw him a couple of weeks ago . . . driving a . . . " His voice trailed away and he gave a quick, guilty glance at his wife.

Joanna stiffened. There was something here, some rekindled hatred . . . she glanced at their faces and read some furtiveness, some concealment. All her senses were jangling.

Andy Carter spoke quickly. "The nurse took a letter to Molly," he said. "He told her *everything* before he jumped."

Joanna sat very still. "And where is Molly now?"

"In a home," Ann Carter said. The atmosphere was beginning to thaw. "She's

265

wheelchair-fast. They look after her well, though. Michael needn't have worried, not like he did. It was all so unnecessary."

All so unnecessary . . . The phrase rang in Joanna's ears all the way home.

14

She was excited when Mike called round in the morning. Late. He always felt he should register his disapproval of working on a Sunday. She'd been pacing in front of the window for more than half an hour, reluctant to call his home. Fran Korpanski hated being bothered by colleagues from the force — at any time — and especially Joanna, especially on a Sunday. So although she had picked up the phone more than once she hadn't even begun dialling his number. It was a relief to hear his tyres scrabbling over the gravel. She flung the door open.

"At last," she said. "I've found a connection between Michael Frost's suicide and Selkirk."

He was out of the car in double-quick time. "What?" he demanded. "How? When?"

"I visited the Carters last night."

"I thought you seemed a bit anxious to get rid of me." He sounded hurt.

"I decided it would be less intimidating."

"Well, go on, then." Korpanski was definitely sulking.

"It's so simple," she said. "Frost's wife was the lollipop lady outside the school. She was injured in the accident, badly injured. She lost both her legs."

Mike stared at her. "Joanna," he said slowly, "where does that leave us?"

"Mike," she said deliberately, "Molly Frost is stuck in a wheelchair. There's no way she could have got to Selkirk. Unless of course she used a hired killer."

Mike was dubious. "I'm not convinced. Why wait all this time? Rowena Carter's accident was five years ago. Her husband committed suicide a year ago. How could she possibly have known Selkirk had been admitted to hospital that morning? And then there's Yolande Prince. Far from dragging her in as an accomplice she's more likely to have blamed the nurse for her husband's death."

"She might have done," she agreed cautiously.

Mike had another objection. "And how is she supposed to have reached a first-floor flat and murdered her? I didn't notice a lift." His eyes were dark as he added, "We both saw Yolande. There's no way someone in a wheelchair could have strangled her."

"There's one way to settle this, Mike." She slammed the door behind her and turned the key. "Let's go and see her after the briefing. Perhaps we'll find out."

★ ★ ★

The briefing had originally been called for ten thirty, out of respect for the 'day of rest'. But before she had time to make her way to the interview room a telephone call came through. It was Pugh and she sounded pleased with herself. "We've got Gallini here," she said, "in custody, and I've quizzed him." She gave one of her loud, barking laughs. "Over and over again, actually. He doesn't seem to want — or to be able — to tell us much, unfortunately." She paused for breath. "I had rather hoped to be able to hand you the whole thing on a plate. Save police time and all that."

"Is he going to tell us anything?"

"Doesn't know a lot," Pugh said. "I got a few things out of him."

Joanna smiled and held the receiver close to her ear. "I thought you said he wouldn't talk."

"We've got our ways." Pugh's laugh sounded hollow.

"You don't mean . . . ?"

"Get up to date," Pugh said. "Your idea, actually. Deals, sentence-bargaining. And just a possibility he'll serve part of his sentence in his beloved Sicily. Though why," she gave an expression of disgust, "why on earth he'd want to go there . . . I've heard the prisons are positively uncivilized."

"Well, ours aren't exactly paradise."

"Quite . . . quite," Pugh said hastily. "Anyway. They used box numbers throughout. And . . . you'll love this. He even has a mobile phone. Quite the little businessman."

"How did they make contact?"

"He didn't want to tell me," Pugh explained, "because it was rather clever. He answered an advert in one of the specialist weaponry magazines. In the wanted column was an advert for an antique assassin's gun. Good price paid and all that. North of England. And for Gallini he showed a glimmer of intelligence. He answered the advert saying he didn't have an antique assassin's gun but he had a modern one in good working order. It would cost ten thousand pounds. He left a mobile phone number, no address."

"So he spoke to someone? Man or a woman?"

"He says a woman." Pugh was irritated at being interrupted. "It was a woman who rang him up on the Monday morning to say there had been a slight change of plan and that Selkirk could be found in the local hospital. This person told him a nurse would let him in through the side door. And I was right about something else," she said proudly. "He spent most of the afternoon wandering round the hospital in various disguises."

"Gosh." Even now Joanna was finding the whole thing incredible. She chewed this latest fact over before remembering Yolande's death.

"You know there was a second murder don't you? The nurse we interviewed the morning after Selkirk's disappearance?"

"Yes," Pugh barked down the phone. "That wasn't Gallini. He was driving back down to London by then. The car was delivered back at the garage by nine o'clock in the morning, waiting outside when they opened. And you'll be pleased to know they couldn't quite clean all the blood off the back seat, even with a most thorough valeting." She chuckled. "Fiat Panda, for your information. Didn't quite do it in style, did he? But, Piercy," she said, "he didn't kill that girl. You'll have to look a little closer to home."

Joanna frowned. "Was his contact definitely a woman?"

"Yes," Pugh said decisively, "according to Gallini." Then, "You did say it was one of the nurses from the hospital who was found dead?"

"Yes. Strangled."

"Ah," said Pugh. "So I was right. An inside job — or at least there was inside involvement."

"Yes."

"I knew someone had to have let him in. The fire door was simply proof for what I already knew. By the way," she added, "you may be interested to know that Gallini in the presence of the nurse told Selkirk they were moving him to another ward. Selkirk thought Gallini was just a porter. Once in the car the gun was jammed against his head. And then his mouth was taped. Oh, and another thing."

Joanna stiffened. Not more ugly facts?

"Gallows Wood wasn't his idea. It was a suggestion made by his employer. They thought it ideal."

"I see. Thanks for letting me know," Joanna said, and suddenly was curious. "What's he like?"

"Our cold-blooded killer?" Pugh sighed. "Not very bright. Knows just enough English to get by. Cold eyes. Very unemotional." She paused. "No pity. There would be no point in appealing to his better nature — he hasn't got one. He's a big man, six feet tall, black hair, wide across the shoulders. Bit like your friend, Sergeant Korpanski. Looks as though he could throw you over his shoulder. But unlike Korpanski he looks as though he'd like to. Not a nice character to have loose on the streets."

Mike stuck his head round the door as Joanna put down the phone. "I thought you'd promised us a briefing this morning."

"A phone call from Pugh," she explained.

"Coming up to visit us again?"

She shook her head. "Not in the foreseeable future."

"Whew, thank God."

"And she was nice about you too. Have you got the report on that letter yet?"

"No."

"Then check it up, Mike, please."

The briefing proved unexpectedly productive. She watched the morale lift as she discussed her recent findings and PC Timmis had a bit of news too. "I paid a visit to Dustin Holloway last night." He looked pleased with himself. "He confessed he'd been after badgers. Of course, we've known that for ages but couldn't get any evidence. But this time we were lucky enough to find a dead one in the back of his car. It had been mauled something rotten."

"Unlucky for the badger," Joanna commented. "Did he see anything at the wood?"

Timmis nodded. "He saw a man walking out. A little after one in the morning. Tall, dark haired, slim. He got into a . . . "

"Don't tell me — a Fiat Panda."

"Yes. Holloway even took the number. Quite the Neighbourhood Watch prodigy." He handed Joanna a sheet of paper. She would match up the number later with that of the hire car. "Holloway says he'll even give evidence if we drop charges."

Joanna stared. "Oh, really," she said. "Well that's mighty big of our Mr Holloway. You can tell him to get stuffed. No deal, and we'll up the badger baiting sentence for attempting to bribe a police officer."

Mike put his hand on her arm. "Steady on, Jo."

She glared at him. "I'm in a mean mood," she said, "fed up with all these petty crooks after bloody deals."

"Well, what about Gallini? You were encouraging Pugh to make a deal with him."

She met his eyes. "Only so we could find out who the real killer was, the person morally responsible for Selkirk's murder."

"Well, hang on a minute," he argued. "Gallini shot him. Whoever it was who killed him just had the money. That wouldn't have killed Selkirk, would it? So they're both equally responsible."

"And what about Yolande Prince?" she

said. "We can't blame our Sicilian friend for her death."

He grinned then. "No," he admitted.

She turned her attention back to the group sitting in the corner. "You've been checking out the flats where Yolande Prince lived?"

They nodded.

"Come up with anything?"

"The next-door neighbour heard her come in," PC Jenkins said. "That was at about twelve midday."

Joanna nodded. "Not long after we'd interviewed her," she said. "Then what?"

"She heard her take a bath. Walls are thin," he explained. "About lunchtime she heard the doorbell ring, three times."

"And?"

"The neighbour was just getting the baby to sleep, so she hoped no one would be making a noise."

"She didn't look to see who it was?"

"No."

"Then what?"

"She heard talking. For about ten minutes. The radio was on low. She couldn't hear much. The radio was turned off a couple of minutes later. Then all was quiet."

Joanna turned her attention to one of the SOC team. "I suppose it's too much to expect that there was a fingerprint on one of the radio controls?"

"Far too much," he said with a smile. "Nothing there."

She sighed and turned back to Jenkins. "Then what?"

"It just went quiet. The baby went to sleep and the neighbour had a bath, watched television. She was just glad of the peace."

"I don't suppose she saw anyone leave the flat?"

"She looked out a couple of minutes after the radio was turned off and thought she saw someone disappearing down the stairs. A man, in a peaked cap and a long dark coat." He paused before adding apologetically, "She only saw the back view."

Joanna drew in a deep breath. "Height?"

"Around five ten, medium build, couldn't see the hair."

"Don't tell me, collar turned up."

Jenkins gave a rueful grin.

"Well," she said. "Thank you. That was the killer. And it was no hired assassin this time, imported from London. That was someone local. Someone from Leek. Someone whom Yolande almost certainly knew. And . . . " she gazed around the room, "the same person who hired Gallini."

Molly Frost lived in a small, single-storey, nursing home. And it was a woman in a wheelchair who answered the door.

"Molly? She's down here." She led them along a bright, sunny corridor towards a closed door at the end. Someone in one of the rooms must have had a radio playing. Joanna could hear the sound of a hymn. She closed her eyes and for an instant was transported back to childhood, the sun streaming through stained-glass windows. She opened her eyes and breathed in the unmistakable scent of the Sunday roast.

Molly Frost was sitting inside, also in a wheelchair. It was then that Joanna really understood the extent of her injuries. And somehow the plaster on her own arm seemed a tiny price to pay for her encounter with the lorry. Molly had been hit by a car. And five years later she was still suffering, and that suffering would never stop.

A deep scar along her cheek, an expression of chronic pain, stiffness in her arm as she gestured for the two detectives to sit down. And that was before Joanna allowed her gaze to wander down to the flatness beneath the blanket.

But Molly Frost was a fighting woman and she met Joanna's gaze without flinching.

"So you're Detective Inspector Piercy," she said, giving a quick glance to the pile of newspapers in the corner.

Joanna nodded.

"I've been reading about you. It seems you've had some success in solving local crime."

"I've had my share of luck," Joanna said guardedly, "so far. But I still don't know what happened this time."

"So you come to me." Her hair was brown, curly and pretty. She stared at Joanna. "A wheelchair-bound woman with no legs and you've come to me?"

Joanna was silent.

Molly Frost gave a deep sigh. "You may have had your share of luck. And I've had more than my share of trouble. I don't mourn Selkirk," she said slowly. "However awful his death, I don't think any of us affected by that dreadful accident could possibly mourn him." She stopped and swallowed. "He took so much. The Carters lost their little daughter. And she was a nice kid. I lost my health and all our happiness too," she said. "Michael took it even worse than I did."

They were interrupted by a nurse walking in briskly. "Time for your morphine, Molly," she said and fiddled with a syringe connected to a tiny plastic pipe.

Molly watched the nurse without emotion. "Morphine," she said calmly. "I have it to control the pain in my smashed spine."

Her eyes burned with an angry light. "And yet, the pain that I go through is nothing compared to what poor Michael suffered."

She stared first at Joanna and then at Mike. "Sometimes," she said, "in my more fanciful moments, I imagine that Michael jumped out of the window so he could be like me, experience what I was living through, twisted and smashed. In pain. Broken. But that wasn't it. He really did want to die." She closed her eyes for a few minutes. Neither of the two police spoke. When she looked at them again it was with a wry sarcasm. "The hospital compensated me, you know." She swallowed. "I was advised to sue for neglect."

"Who handled the case?"

Molly Frost gave a painful twist to her face. "Not Selkirk," she said. "Another firm, O'Donnell's." Her face hardened. "'Make them pay,' he said, and got me legal aid to do it."

"How much was the award?"

"Twelve thousand pounds." Molly Frost was fighting to regain control now. "For Michael. It was the final insult." She stopped, blinked. Tears rolled down her cheeks. "Anyway, you didn't come here to listen to my life story, did you?" There was a shrewd, calculating look in her eyes. "You probably know it already."

Joanna nodded.

Molly Frost gazed at her boldly. "Why *did* you come?"

Joanna leaned closer, met the woman's straight gaze. "What's the connection between your husband's suicide and Selkirk's murder, Mrs Frost?"

She looked surprised. "Is there a connection?"

"We don't know." Joanna decided to lob the ball straight into Molly Frost's side of the court. "What do you think?"

"I'd like to think so," Molly said. "I really would. For that sweet little girl, Rowena . . . for my poor, lost legs. And most of all for Michael's life. I'd love to think that pig's murder was some small downpayment for them. Unfortunately I don't know." She fiddled with the blanket that should have covered her legs. "Tell me, Inspector." She swivelled the chair round to face Joanna. "The accident that broke your arm. Would you like revenge?"

"How did you . . . ?"

"It was in the local paper. So tell me. Would you?"

And by comparing injuries Joanna had an inkling of what the two families had been through. She nodded dumbly.

Molly Frost was waiting for her reply. "Someone shot him, didn't they?"

"Someone was paid to shoot him," Mike corrected brutally.

"And you think it was me?"

Neither police officer said a word.

Molly sank back. "I see," she said slowly.

"Did you have any contact with Yolande Prince after your husband's suicide?"

Molly Frost might have pretended she didn't know who Yolande Prince was. Instead she nodded. "The poor little nurse. She didn't let us down, did she?" She looked at Mike. "I spoke to her after Michael died. She felt guilty." She hesitated, uncertain whether or not to speak the next sentence. "She felt it was her fault."

"Because she didn't give him his drugs the night Michael died?"

Molly nodded. "I told her I was the cause of his unhappiness, not her. She always promised she would do anything she could to help." Her face changed. "And it seems she must have done."

"What do you mean?" Joanna asked quietly.

Molly shifted in her wheelchair. "She had something to do with it, didn't she?"

"How do you know?"

"The Carters told me she was found dead.

I'd read she'd been on duty in the hospital that night and put two and two together. The Carters have been very good," she said defensively. "They've become real friends. They often visit. And when they can't come in they ring me." She motioned the telephone on the locker. "We have a lot in common. I was with their daughter of course when . . . " And even now Molly Frost couldn't complete the sentence.

Joanna watched Mike's shoulders slump. But she still needed to probe.

"What did your husband say in his final letter?"

"It's none of your business." Molly was angry now. "It was personal. Between me and Michael. For no one else's eyes. And just for the record," she said, "I had nothing to do with Jonathan Selkirk's murder."

★ ★ ★

They sat in Joanna's office drinking coffee, contemplating each suspect one by one.

"I don't suppose the bank accounts have made things any easier for us?" she said hopefully.

Mike shook his head. "No large amounts moved from any of them."

"Oh well, I thought not. That would be

too easy." She leaned forward, cupped her chin in her hand. "So what do you think about Molly?"

Mike's dark eyes were watching her. "She could have hired the killer."

He nodded. "She could," he agreed, guardedly.

"In fact," Joanna pursued, "she would *have* to have hired a killer. Because she couldn't have done it herself."

"Why wait?" he objected. "Her accident, her husband's suicide. They all happened a long time ago. Why wait until now?"

"Money, possibly," she suggested. "She's just had all that compensation."

"But she couldn't have killed Yolande."

Joanna shook her head. "No. That's what's bothering me. She fits in some ways. In others . . . No, you're right. She couldn't have killed her, nor would she have wanted to. Her bitterness was solely for Selkirk. And she didn't strike me as a malicious woman."

"But Yolande was only involved because of Selkirk's heart attack. And didn't Pugh say something about Gallini never changing a day? Wasn't it that night or never?"

"I still can't see her planning the whole thing with Yolande, pretending he was to be punished, frightened. There's something so much more vindictive, clever, even, about

283

that. And it doesn't seem like Molly Frost."

They were both silent for a moment before Joanna added slowly, "But Yolande would have done her bidding, wouldn't she?"

They both sat and thought of the small, plump woman confined to a wheelchair after that one, horrible accident. Both were anxious to move on to another suspect.

"I suppose we'd better consider the Carters — both of them. Andy I don't suspect," Joanna said slowly. "When he said he wouldn't have hired someone else to kill Selkirk I believed him. It held the ring of truth. He would have done it himself, five years ago, as just revenge for his daughter. And hang the consequences. I don't see him planning something like this, Mike. Still less involving the nurse who had absolutely no connection with the Carter case. And again, why wait? If anything, their pain has dulled over the years, hasn't it?"

"But there's always Mrs Carter."

Joanna drained her cup of coffee and set it down on the desk. "I suppose so," she said. "She's a possibility, but could she get her hands on ten thousand pounds?"

Mike stood up, paced around the room, came to a halt in front of the desk. And as always she was uncomfortably aware of the burly policeman.

"Sit down, for goodness' sake," she said irritably. "You make me nervous pacing around like a caged tiger."

He dropped into the armchair, protesting. "I don't know how you can sit there, contemplating," he complained, "just rolling the pencil between your fingers."

She tapped her forehead. "All the work's done inside here," she said, laughing. "I'm working just as hard. It's just that you can't see it."

He grinned too.

"Come on," she said. "Let's try and put some logic behind our thinking. Whoever planned all this was ruthless enough to want Selkirk dead, so much so that the nurse was simply a disposable means to an end. So we're looking here at a powerful hatred in a strong character."

"What about Pritchard?"

She made a face. "Grandpa Tony? He might have hired a killer for Selkirk," she said. "He strikes me as the sort of man who wouldn't want to get his hands dirty. The point is, Mike, could he have persuaded Yolande Prince to take Selkirk out of the hospital? Would she have let him visit her flat to explain?"

"I don't think so, Jo."

"They didn't even know each other. And

besides, what was in it for him?"

"Marry Selkirk's widow? She's worth plenty of money."

Joanna nodded. It was a possibility. "And another thing, Mike. He knew Selkirk was in hospital, didn't he?"

"So is he top of the list?"

"What do you think?"

"I can't see it somehow." He paused, scowling. "I can't picture him planning the whole thing so cleverly."

"And neither can I. So who does that leave us with?"

"I suppose the rest of the family," he said slowly. "Wife, son, daughter-in-law?"

"And the wife at least had the lot, didn't she? Opportunity and money. But I can't think why."

Mike laughed. "Maybe they just didn't like him very much."

"Seems a good enough reason," she said with a smile, then added thoughtfully, "what if the dislike went deeper than we realized?"

"What do you mean?" He looked questioningly at her.

"I don't quite know," she confessed. "It's just a vague idea at the moment."

"But she was quite open about not grieving for Selkirk."

"I know. But sometimes," she said slowly,

"people conceal things with half-truths."

"I'm sorry?"

"She said she didn't like him. She didn't say she hated him, did she?"

"Well, no. She didn't."

"His son certainly didn't hate him," she said. "He feared him. And as for the pregnant Teresa I got the distinct impression she was indifferent to her father-in-law."

"Not to Mrs Selkirk, though. They all seemed . . . "

"To cluster around her for guidance?"

Mike nodded.

"And lastly," she said, "we have that sweet character Wilde."

Mike's response was simply one word. "Why?"

"Well . . . " she said slowly " . . . he thought the Fraud Squad might drop the case if his partner was dead."

"Weak," Mike objected. "That's very weak."

She sighed. "It is, isn't it?" She looked up a second later. "His daughter, the Barbie doll?"

"Again, why?" He raised his eyebrows.

"What if she planned the whole thing, Mike, strung him along, convincing him to give her money before setting up Gallini to despatch Selkirk. I can see her typing the

287

threat. And what's more, I can picture her visiting Yolande at her flat, too. What do you think of that for a theory?"

"I suppose it's possible. And she was supposed to be his adoring mistress. That's the trouble with this job," he grumbled. "It destroys your faith in human nature. Especially women." Joanna's face softened with amusement. "You know," she said, "I like the idea of it being Miss Wilde."

"Sadist."

"What's her first name?"

"Can't you guess?" Mike grinned. "Samantha."

"So how am I doing, Mike?"

"Not bad," he said, "for someone with a broken arm."

"So tomorrow," she promised, "we'll pay a few visits."

Mike moved towards the door. "You want a lift home?"

She shook her head. "I'll stay here for a bit. I want to do some more thinking."

"About Wilde?"

"No, about Selkirk."

He closed the door gently.

She sat very still for a moment. Selkirk had been a despicable character. Almost all he had touched had been warped by him. He had ruined the lives of two families and escaped unscathed through what he would have considered cleverness. When he had mown down Rowena Carter on the school crossing he had not thought of her, or of her family. There had been no remorse. He had thought only to save his own skin.

Yolande Prince's connection with Selkirk had been tenuous. She had been a shining nurse, loved by her family; her decency had been part of her. But there had been that one great trauma in her life, Michael Frost's suicide. It had clouded the judgement of a warm, devoted person and his death could also be lain at Selkirk's door. And that had proved to be Yolande's own destruction too because it had left her with a weak spot which had been ruthlessly exploited.

But by whom?

15

The station was eerily quiet that afternoon. Joanna was alone with the empty desks and blank computer screens, the piles of papers and chalked boards — all the debris of a major investigation.

Matthew would be spending the day with Eloise and the knowledge made her feel even more excluded. So she prowled between the rows with a feeling of loneliness mounting inside her until she called a taxi to take her home.

But even that was a mistake. At home she felt restless and fidgety, unable to settle all evening. One-handed, she managed to boil the kettle and make coffee, but preparing much of a meal was beyond her.

What would she do with the luxury of a second hand? The plaster had become part of her, its heaviness hardly noticeable, even its bulk felt normal. The flashbacks of lorry wheels spinning towards her were fading. In the excitement of a murder inquiry the accident had receded into the background, but would it emerge as soon as she rode her bike again?

She switched on the television. Luckily there was a lively play on, good enough to distract her from the case. Two glasses of red wine and an hour and a half later she was sleepy enough for bed. But once there she tossed and turned, her thoughts drifting from her own accident to Selkirk's death, then on to the murder of the nurse. At about two a.m. she sat up.

* * *

Mike turned up faithfully at eight thirty in the morning and quickly sensed something was on her mind. As soon as she was in the car he challenged her.

"Come on, what is it?"

"The Merry Widow," she said grimly. "I keep coming back to her. Why didn't she leave him? Why did she stay? She didn't have to. She was a professional woman and it wasn't as though he shared a close relationship with his son."

"Why do *you* think she stayed?"

"The only reason I've come up with that holds any water is his money. And habit — security. I can't prove it, Mike, she said, "but I can build up a very convincing case against her. The whole thing seemed to fit into place at about two this morning."

He laughed. "So a flash of inspiration has solved it?"

Gravely she shook her head. "No, just raised a few more observations. She was prepared to tolerate Selkirk until he managed to find himself a mistress — of sorts. She must have thought herself quite safe from that threat at least, but Selkirk managed to surprise her even on that count. She'll have worried she would lose everything. After all those years."

"Maybe." Mike was dubious. "But I would have thought she was the sort of woman who'd something a bit cleverer than simply hire a killer to do the job. She could have used poison, fiddled with the car. Something," he finished lamely.

She shot him an amused glance. "And I thought I was the one with a degree in psychology."

"OK," he said. "You're the clever inspector while I'm the stupid sergeant."

She whisked her head towards him, never quite sure how much truth there was behind these seemingly idle jests. His face was expressionless.

"There are a few more avenues of enquiry that would bear closer scrutiny," she said steadily.

"Such as?"

"The letter, Mike. What was the purpose of it? Could she have sent it? Where the hell is that report?"

"I'll chase it." He put a restraining hand on her arm. "Don't jump to conclusions."

"Well, we do know that after three years it disturbed him enough to bring on a heart attack."

"It could have been coincidence."

"Come on, Mike." She didn't even argue the point with him. "Then again, what part exactly did Yolande play? Was she an innocent dupe?" She screwed her face up. "I can't believe she was so stupid as to have anything to do with the abduction of her patient. But what alternative do we have?"

Mike shrugged.

"You see, I still fail to cast her in a completely guilty role. She can't have known Selkirk was to be shot." She turned to face him. "Although I can imagine Sheila planning the whole thing, I can't see Yolande being so stupid." She recalled the earnest, honest face with its clear complexion.

Mike was silent and she watched him overtake a parked car whose door was suddenly flung wide open before she continued. "And while I'm about it, Mike, there are other things puzzling me."

He risked a swift glance at her. "Such as?"

"How did Andy Carter know Selkirk had been forced to kneel before he was shot?"

Mike's profile stiffened.

"And why is a photograph of Rowena Carter missing?"

Again Mike shrugged. "Could mean anything. Maybe it needed new glass or a different frame."

"Maybe."

"Well, ask them."

"I think I might." She shook her head. "Almost a week into the case, Mike, and we still don't know much, do we?"

"We've got Gallini."

Her face twisted. "Pugh's got Gallini and she knew he was responsible almost before she got here. That's not exactly something we can take credit for."

His face darkened. "So where now?"

"Let's pay a little surprise visit to the Selkirk homestead."

★ ★ ★

The Selkirks' drive was jammed with cars. Pritchard's Jaguar was there, Sheila's Peugeot, and Justin's old banger. They threaded between them.

Joanna touched the Jaguar. "He's got

expensive tastes, hasn't he?" It was the only remark she made.

Mike's rejoinder was crisp. "All these cars," he said. "They're having a party. I don't bloody believe it."

"Call it a reunion of a family."

The autumn sunshine made the old house glow. The windows caught the light and threw out flames of celebration. The front door stood half open. Mike gave a very soft knock and they walked straight in.

The family was in conference, Pritchard and Sheila sitting together on the sofa, Justin in the corner, Teresa perched on the piano stool and the child sitting in the middle of the floor. It was the child who saw them first. She regarded them gravely but said nothing.

Sheila Selkirk must have caught the movement from the doorway. She whisked her head round, startled.

"We did knock," Joanna said pleasantly. "You can't have heard us."

There was a remarkable stillness in the room, a stage tableau where everyone was frozen. Even the child seemed to stop breathing.

Pritchard was the first to come back to life. "Now look here . . . " He began his bluff.

As usual Sheila Selkirk pulled no punches. "Do you know what the total arsehole's done now?" she demanded. Without waiting for a reply she continued. "I shall contest, of course."

Joanna guessed. "It wouldn't be anything to do with a will, would it?" It seemed the only means of her husband's exerting any influence over her now.

Sheila Selkirk looked at her suspiciously. "You knew?"

"We hadn't got round to checking it. That was just a wild guess."

Surprisingly it was Justin who spoke up next, breathing hard down his nostrils. "After the devastation of my father's brutal and merciless murder," he began in his nasal whine, "he has hit us," he said, flinging out his arms, "from beyond the grave."

At the sudden movement the child flinched.

Joanna spoke briskly. "Would anyone like to tell me what's happened?"

It was left to Sheila Selkirk. "That absolute bastard. You'll never guess where he's left his money."

Joanna raised her eyebrows.

"To that po-faced, painted bimbo," she said, "that affected, lying little bitch. If I ever get my hands around her neck. Winding her legs round my husband."

Mike moved forward. "Just for the record, Mrs Selkirk, what would you do when you had your hands around her neck?"

For the first time Sheila Selkirk hesitated, seemed to realize what she was saying. She recovered herself quickly. "I shall contest," she repeated. "Even if her father is a bloody solicitor. So am I." She glared at Joanna. "For your information, Inspector, and before you hear it elsewhere, my husband decided to leave his money — *all* of his money — to the Wilde spawn, the woman who masquerades as his mistress."

Her eyes moved around the room, "Thank God I have my family," she said quietly and with surprising dignity.

Right on cue Teresa Selkirk struggled to her feet. She moved towards Sheila, put her arms around her and pressed her cheek against Sheila's face.

Joanna could almost hear the stage direction. This happy family was about as real as the cardboard game. There was a strong scent of manipulation. But who was manipulating whom?

Justin seemed to feel some explanation was necessary. "After the awful events and the . . . " he passed a hand across his brow, "simply disgusting conditions my own family was forced to accept," he said, "my mother invited us to come and live with her."

Sheila nodded. "And as soon as the dust

has settled," she gave a fond glance at Pritchard, "Tony and I will get married."

Pritchard stared at the floor.

"The dust won't settle, Mrs Selkirk," Joanna took great delight in the title, "until your husband's killer has been brought to justice."

Sheila Selkirk gave a smug smile. "But you already have him, don't you? The Italian?"

"We have him, Mrs Selkirk," Mike said. "We don't have the person who paid him to murder your husband, and we don't have the person responsible for the murder of Yolande Prince — yet."

"Oh, the nurse." Sheila looked bored.

"Yes, the nurse," Joanna echoed.

Something in Sheila's eyes flickered. She swallowed. "Look," she said irritably, "you saw the letter Jonathan received that precipitated his heart attack. He'd had them before. It's obvious the whole business was connected with that unfortunate little girl he knocked down." The family all nodded in agreement.

"We're certainly pursuing all enquiries," Joanna said calmly. "So, while I'm here, where were you all on Tuesday?"

"I was here," Sheila said first, "as you well know. I stayed here all bloody day, waiting for news of my husband." She had great difficulty saying the words.

"Mr Selkirk?"

"I was at work. Lots of people saw me."

"People like Lou-lou?" Mike was having trouble keeping his face straight.

"She, and others," Justin said haughtily. The public school education hadn't been a complete waste of money, then. He could still turn on the autocrat. For the second time Joanna had caught a glimpse of his father in him. It was no prettier a sight this time round.

Teresa flicked a length of cigarette ash into the dish. "I was at an ante-natal appointment," she volunteered quietly, "at the hospital."

"What time was your appointment, Mrs Selkirk?"

"Eleven o'clock, but you're there all bloody day. Ask any of the midwives." She ground out her cigarette and gave the police officers a secretive smile.

"And you, Mr Pritchard?"

"Golf." He gave an embarrassed laugh. "Round of golf, lunch, another round of golf. Plenty of witnesses."

Joanna frowned. How the hell did Tony Pritchard make his living?

"Why are you asking about Tuesday?" Sheila barked. "My husband was dragged from his hospital bed on Monday, in the night."

"And the nurse was strangled a couple of hours after talking to us on Tuesday morning," Mike put in.

Joanna studied the ring of faces. They were waiting and watching. Alert like little foxes who hear the distant baying of hounds. Ready to start running and dodging. Even the child had scrambled to her feet now and was leaning slightly forward as though waiting for the starter's pistol.

The thought flashed through Joanna's mind. They had all wanted Selkirk dead. Everyone in this room had hated him. The question was, had any one of them wanted him dead enough?

Justin Selkirk, with his pale face, bent shoulders, nervous, twitching eyes? Had he been the one to tease his father with that letter?

Joanna's eyes swivelled round to take in the calm, Madonna-like Teresa, her hands still cradling her unborn child. Had she hated her father-in-law enough to arrange for a killer to visit him, showing no pity even after he'd suffered a heart attack?

And Sheila Selkirk, with her strong, confident features, so sure of herself except in the area of her marriage.

Tony Pritchard, a man Joanna suspected of having expensive tastes without the visible means to pay for them?

For sure, none of them would betray the other. There was tangible solidarity in this room that even extended to the child, Lucy, now sitting quietly on the floor, her saucer eyes fixed on Joanna.

She cast around for some wedge to divide the family. Surely that was the answer — to somehow separate their individual self-interest? In desperation she lunged blindly. "Did you know Michael Frost?"

"We didn't know him." Sheila spoke angrily for all of them. "We knew who he was. This is a small town, Inspector Piercy. Bad news travels. The entire Carter case was given full coverage for a second time. His suicide gave rise to yet another avalanche of lurid headlines . . . second tragedy and all that."

She dismissed them with the tilt of her head. "We knew the name, nothing more. Certainly not one of us ever met the man." There was not a trace of emotion towards the dead man or his predicament even though her own husband had been indirectly responsible. Joanna would gain nothing here.

She gave up. "Well, thank you, all of you," she said pleasantly. "It's been most interesting."

16

They sat outside the house for a full five minutes before Mike made his comment. "Well, that was a right waste of time, wasn't it?"

"Really, Mike?" She raised her eyebrows mockingly. "I'm surprised at you. We've learned something all right. We've learned where Jonathan Selkirk left his money, haven't we?"

"And what does that tell us?"

"Well, it's worth following up at least."

He started up the engine.

Selkirk & Wilde looked no less prosperous today than it had on their first visit, with its elegant, Georgian façade.

"It looks about the last place on earth to be investigated by the Fraud Squad," Mike remarked.

"Which only proves how deceptive appearances can be." Joanna pushed open the door.

Apparently the death of one of its partners had not had a detrimental effect on business. A couple were sitting in the foyer facing Samantha.

She was no longer dressed in mourning but in a scarlet miniskirt and lots of gold jewellery.

She met Joanna's eyes boldly.

"I feel I ought to congratulate you, Miss Wilde," Joanna said smoothly, "on your excellent fortune. Now can we go somewhere private, please, to talk?"

The blonde's eyes flickered and suddenly she looked younger, less sure of herself. And Joanna wondered how big a part Daddy had played in her luck. She led the two officers to a small ante room.

"Tell me, how much do you think your inheritance is worth?"

"I don't know. I really haven't a clue." Her innocent eyes met Joanna's. "I didn't think . . . Not for a moment. It was a complete surprise."

"I'm sure."

The girl pouted. Sticky red lips dropped. From beauty to the grotesque in one swift move. Joanna watched her curiously. Glamour, not beauty, had been this girl's calling card. She was not a natural. She would need that money.

The girl blinked. "Mrs Selkirk . . . " she began.

"Ah yes, Mrs Selkirk," Joanna said. "I don't think she's very pleased with you."

Mike spoke from behind her. "Says you were having it off with her husband."

The girl was quick to defend her honour. "No," she protested. "No, absolutely not. We never did."

"Just a little harmless flirtation?" Joanna ploughed on ruthlessly. "Titillation?"

"You've no right to say that." Rufus Wilde was standing in the doorway, wearing a threatening solicitor's hard face. "If you're insinuating . . . "

"I'm just curious." Joanna said, "about why Jonathan Selkirk left all his money to your daughter." She was past caring about people's feelings. "What was she giving him that was worth so much?"

"I don't like your tone, Inspector." Wilde's eyes narrowed. "He was fond of her. We were far more of a family to him than ever his own were. He liked my daughter."

"Liked?" Mike's jaw squared. "I like lots of people," he said. "I wouldn't dream of leaving them my money."

Joanna cleared her throat. "You see, Mr and Miss Wilde." And again she was reminded of the game of Happy Families. Mr and Miss Wilde. But they wouldn't be cast as solicitors, would they? "Selkirk leaving all his money to you is an anomaly," she paused, "if you were no more to each other than friends. After all, this is a double murder we are investigating."

Father looked at daughter.

"Did you know Mr Selkirk was intending to leave his money to you?"

She shook her head and couldn't resist a swift glance at her father. For what? — approval?

He gave an almost imperceptible nod.

"And where were you both the morning of last Tuesday?"

"Here," they answered swiftly in unison.

Rufus Wilde cleared his throat. "With Jonathan in hospital we had a lot of extra work here," he explained. "Someone had to manage the business."

"Ah yes," Joanna said. "The business." She watched Rufus Wilde carefully. "The business currently under investigation by the Serious Fraud Office. Tell me, Mr Wilde, as a solicitor. If Mrs Selkirk were to contest her husband's will, would she stand a chance of winning the case?"

He cleared his throat. "My daughter had considered making some sort of a settlement . . . " he began.

"To shut her up?" Joanna said sharply. "Just answer the question, please."

"Under current law," the solicitor began, "a person's will is carried out, unless it can

305

be proved he or she was of unsound mind when making out the will."

Joanna derived some satisfaction from the fact that Rufus Wilde was patently uncomfortable. Good. It suited her.

"And was he?" Mike asked brusquely.

Wilde stared at them. He opened his mouth to speak, then shut it again.

"I see," Joanna said pleasantly. "The three monkeys — see, hear, say nothing. But we both know, don't we, Mr Wilde? Selkirk was not of unsound mind when he made that will and you know it will be contested in a court of law, don't you?"

Wilde nodded.

"A wife can surely claim half, can't she? So any sum you gave Sheila Selkirk would be a token — nothing else — something to try to keep her away from the courts." Joanna thought for a minute, her brain working overtime. "And of course your daughter, I presume, is an employee of Selkirk & Wilde rather than a partner. And as such could not be liable for the firm's debts of corruption. Neat trick," she said blandly. "Provided Jonathan Selkirk's assets were not seized by the SFO."

"Now look here." Wilde was rattled now. Joanna could not suppress a quick, triumphant grin at Mike. "Jonathan was entitled to leave his money wherever he liked," Rufus Wilde said. "He chose to leave it to my daughter, someone he had grown very fond of in the course of his work."

The blonde was blinking rapidly, her head turning from one to the other in an attempt to follow the conversation.

"When was the will dated, Mr Wilde?"

"Last month," Wilde said a little less confidently.

"I see. Well, thank you very much. You've been a great help."

"Is that all?" Wilde demanded. "I've got a business to run."

"Yes, that's all." But she couldn't resist a Parthian shot. "Good luck with the SFO," she said. "I've heard they like to cook their pound of flesh before they eat it." She didn't even look back to see what effect her words had had but left the doors swinging behind her.

She felt good.

They headed back to the station.

Joanna settled behind her desk and spoke to Mike and Dawn Critchlow. "I've plenty of ideas now," she said. "I'd just like one more detail. Have we got the forensic report on the letter sent to Wilde the morning he died?"

He handed it to her. "Arrived this

morning," he said. "Confirmed it was done on a different machine from the original letters. That's the official verdict."

"Good," Joanna smiled. "I was hoping it would be."

She had both their attentions now. "The boys have done a bit of probing into Justin Selkirk's financial affairs. He sold his house six months ago."

"Negative equity," Mike muttered, but Dawn had something up her sleeve.

"That isn't true," she said. "He sold the house for thirty-eight thousand pounds. His mortgage was only thirty."

Joanna gaped. "But . . . " She was conjuring up the sordid, cramped interior of the caravan.

"You tell me," Dawn said, "but according to Constable Phil Scott there aren't eight thousand pounds in his bank account now."

"Well, well, well." Mike looked pleased. "Looks like we have someone wriggling in the bag."

Joanna shot him a warning glance.

Dawn hesitated before pulling something out from behind her back. "There's something else you should see. I saw it at the local newsagent's."

She dropped a magazine on the desk. A woman's magazine with a photograph on the front of a pretty, laughing child. Slashed across the picture was a caption. Rowena Carter, five years old, another child killed by a drunk driver. And underneath in smaller black letters was added, *And he got away with it — or did he? Read inside for full story.*

Joanna looked up. "So that's where the picture of Rowena Carter had disappeared to. I was wondering."

She opened the magazine. The article bore Ann Carter's name at the bottom, a picture of her tearful face, her husband's arms wrapped around her. Joanna read through the article twice. There was a certain tone to it, gloating, malicious but less vindictive than she would have imagined. At the end was a picture of Selkirk and a brief description of the events at Gallows Wood. The last sentence contained the predictable words, 'just deserts'.

Joanna flicked to the front of the magazine. It had come out that day. Thoughtfully she passed it to Mike. He read it without comment. She stood up, unhooked her coat from the back of the chair, draped it round her shoulders. She was getting quite adept at coping with the plaster cast. It had become less of an encumbrance as the days had moved on.

"So we've got the answer to at least one of our questions," she said. "That's where the photograph went. Funny, isn't it?" she said. "That first day we met them it was already written on the wall, as it were." Neither Korpanski nor Dawn had the faintest idea what Joanna was talking about.

She stared at them. "You don't see, do you? Come on, Korpanski, I should buy you lunch. As a chauffeur you haven't been bad."

They were almost through the door when the telephone rang. She was in two minds whether to pick it up. Her conscience won.

"Am I speaking to Detective Inspector Piercy?"

"You are, Mr Prince."

His voice was strong and steady. People had their own ways of dealing with grief. "We feel we must speak up for our daughter," he began. "The newspapers are making suggestions."

Joanna didn't even try to apologize for the tabloids' excesses. The reporters were an intelligent pack, on the whole, and they had scented blood the moment Yolande's death had been made public. They had soon started speculating with their talent for making suppositions sound like facts.

"She wouldn't have done it," he said.

310

"We knew our daughter extremely well. She was protective towards anyone in her care, no matter what their past was. She didn't discriminate."

Joanna's instinct was to discount a fond father's assessment of his daughter's character, but there was no emotion behind his statement. This was a statement of fact.

Mr Prince spoke again. "I suggest, Inspector," he said quietly, "that you stop blaming my daughter for the abduction of Mr Selkirk and look instead at the other nurses on duty that night. My daughter," he said with dignity, "has been made a scapegoat."

* * *

"So what do you think, Mike?" Joanna had relayed the conversation to Mike. Her desk was littered with the contents of all the files connected with the case. Her computer screen was switched on. She had finished leafing through all the statements.

Mike's square face was pensive.

"If Yolande's father is right it would put the case under a different light, wouldn't it?"

He nodded slowly.

She leaned forward, her elbow making a

dent in the cover of the magazine. "I think we're getting closer. Let's visit Emily Place and see if we can get an answer to our second question. Then we'll do a bit of talking."

Mike stood up, towering over her.

"We've nearly got them," she said.

His eyebrows almost met in the middle. "Proof?"

"We'll play one off against the other. There won't be any trust between them, only fear."

* * *

Emily Place looked quiet and dull in the middle of the day. No one was there. There was no sign of life at all.

Except at number fourteen.

Andy Carter was painting an upstairs windowframe. He saw them from the top of the ladder. "Bloody hell, aren't you done with us yet?" he exclaimed.

"Just two more questions, Mr Carter."

He stepped down the ladder, made no attempt to invite them inside.

"You've raked it all up," he said resentfully. "Ann hasn't had a wink of sleep since you first came."

"*We* didn't rake it up," Joanna said quietly.

"We weren't the ones to shoot Selkirk. Once he'd been shot we had no option but to pursue our investigations until we found the perpetrator. Understand?"

Carter blinked. "I suppose you're only doing your job. What was it you wanted to know?"

"How did you know Selkirk had been forced to kneel before he was shot?"

Carter looked rattled. His eyes bounced from Joanna to Mike and back to Joanna again.

"Come on, Carter," Mike urged.

Carter pressed his lips together.

"Then we'll have to take you down to the station for further questioning."

"No, no. I have to be here. Ann'll go mad if I aren't here when she gets home."

The two officers waited and finally Carter relented. "I've got a mate," he said. "He sometimes wanders up those woods. He saw him, lying on his side, his hands tied behind his back."

Joanna let out a long sigh. Another piece of the puzzle had slipped into place.

"Your mate's name wouldn't happen to be Holloway, would it?"

"I can't tell you that," Carter was defensive, "but it's the truth." He turned his back on them. But Joanna waited until the penny dropped and Carter turned around again. "And the other question?"

"I suppose in the last five years you've bought yourselves a new word processor?"

A sharp indrawn breath was the only sign that Carter had heard. "Leave us alone."

"Where is your wife, Mr Carter?"

"Where do you think? She's at work."

★ ★ ★

It was an extraordinary sight, the bright, fluorescent green coat, the huge lollipop, STOP, Children Crossing. They watched her for a few minutes, painfully aware of what she was doing.

A crowd of children gathered at the side of the road. Ann Carter waited. A car approached, slowly. She waited . . . another approached, gathered speed, determined not to be halted.

The car hurtled towards her. Herding the children back on to the pavement, she stepped boldly out. The car screeched to a stop. Two fingers appeared over the driving wheel.

Ann Carter smiled.

The children crossed.

They met her back on the pavement.

She frowned. "Why have you come here?"

Joanna said nothing but watched her steadily.

The woman's eyes slid away from the two officers and towards the traffic belting along the road and the waiting clusters of mothers and children. "I should go to them," she said.

Joanna put a hand on her arm. "I think you should come with us."

17

Mike radioed in for a constable to cover the crossing and they drove Ann Carter to the station. She neither argued nor complained. Neither, they noticed, did she ask them to ring her husband. While he had worried about her returning from work to an empty house she had no thought for him. As they watched the thin, tense face they both knew her mind was still with her daughter.

The first real breakthrough came after half an hour during which she had been silent. Quite suddenly she said very quietly, "I watched him get into the ambulance, you know."

"I thought you might have done." And Joanna at last voiced the one thought that had drawn her back to Ann Carter. "I suppose you had to send the letter didn't you?"

Her answer was a wry shake of the head.

"It was the only thing that could force him to realize the connection with Rowena."

Dumbly Ann Carter nodded. Tears streamed down her face. "He had to know."

"It took you so long to save the money up?"

Ann Carter smiled. "I decided the fates should choose," she said calmly. "Like the National Lottery. Either I would be knocked down or Selkirk would die." She gave a pathetic shake of her head. "It didn't really matter which." Then she stared at Joanna. "I've got nothing left now."

Joanna touched her shoulder briefly. "Let's get you a solicitor, Mrs Carter."

★ ★ ★

Mike followed her up the corridor.

"So the letters?"

"Were written by the same hand but on different machines. The wording, Mike, it was the same. Forensics will never replace good human common sense."

"But what about the nurse? She didn't kill her, did she?"

Joanna turned to face him. "You must be joking," she said.

"Then who?"

She waited until she was safely ensconced in her office before answering. "O'Sullivan," she said. "He was greedy enough to take the money, and hang on to it. He knew Yolande would put two and two together and realize he had let Gallini in."

Mike sank down into the chair. "But why?"

317

"Why what?" Relief at solving the case was making her light-hearted. "Why did he do it? For money. Remember the Carter family were friendly with the Frosts. They would almost certainly have visited Michael Frost in hospital. O'Sullivan was a nurse on the ward where Michael Frost was, as well as Yolande. They would have met them both.

"When Selkirk received the letter, Ann Carter was watching outside. She must have panicked when the ambulance took him to hospital. She rang Gallini and then must have contacted O'Sullivan and enlisted his help. Unfortunately O'Sullivan was astute enough to realize somebody would piece together the fact that Gallini had had help. Cleverly he worked out that strangling Yolande would divert suspicion from him. It would make us think that Yolande had let Gallini in, not him. And we nearly fell for it. It nearly worked."

Mike stared at her. "Proof," he said and she repeated her earlier words.

"We'll play one off against the other. There won't be any trust between them, only fear."

She glanced at the door. "Ann Carter will spill the beans," she said confidently, "in the end. Once we explain the full facts about Yolande. She doesn't lack a conscience. Unlike O'Sullivan. In fact," she said, "there's only one thing bothering me now. What the hell did Justin Selkirk do with all that money?"

Mike was laughing. "I could make an inspired guess."

She eyed him curiously. "Go on."

"That place where he works. All that scaffolding. I bet he's lent Lou-lou some money for renovations." As always when he spoke the woman's name he had difficulty controlling his laughter. This time he didn't bother.

The rest of the force listened to the sound of uncontrolled laughter coming from Joanna's office.

Dawn spoke for them all. "They must have cracked it."

18

A few weeks later Joanne's plaster cast was removed. Her arm looked unfamiliar, white and wasted. She flexed her wrist stiffly.

Tomorrow she could use her bike again.

★ ★ ★

The station was deserted. Most of the officers involved in the murders had taken advantage of some warm autumn sunshine to take back the hours owed. She found Mike sitting at his desk, drinking coffee and checking a pile of statements.

"The case is going to need a stronger prosecution than this," he said. "The proof is flimsy. Basically O'Sullivan denies the lot and Ann Carter's conviction relies on her confession."

"We'll get there, Mike. We've unearthed Gallini's phone print-out. She used the call box at the end of the street. But to ring O'Sullivan she made the mistake of using her own telephone. When we question O'Sullivan we can use that as a lever. We know exactly what time they spoke and for how long. That should help a bit."

"I hope you're right, Jo." Then he noticed her arm. "You've lost your plaster."

"And gained an arm."

She perched on the side of his desk and gave a tentative smile. "She must have planned this whole business all those years ago because Selkirk had killed her daughter and had got off scot free. Love for a child," she said diffidently. "It's a strong thing, isn't it?"

Mike's dark eyes watched her fidget with the pens on his desk. "Are we talking about Rowena Carter," he asked flatly, "or Eloise Levin?" He looked beyond her towards the window. "Because I'm never quite sure with you."

"Both," she said idly, refusing to meet his gaze. She hesitated before plunging on. "I never realized how strong family ties can be."

When Mike had left she picked up the telephone. She'd seen the hotel last year on a drive near Stratford-upon-Avon and thought it looked a perfect retreat for a break — a half-timbered sixteenth-century coaching inn, boasting Egon Ronay recommended food and four-posters in every room. She dialled the number.

"I'd like to book a double room, please, for next weekend . . . "

She put down the phone with a sense of relief.

The struggle was over.

THE END

McLEAN AT THE GOLDEN OWL
George Goodchild

Inspector McLean has resigned from Scotland Yard's CID and has opened an office in Wimpole Street. With the help of his able assistant, Tiny, he solves many crimes, including those of kidnapping, murder and poisoning.

KATE WEATHERBY
Anne Goring

Derbyshire, 1849: The Hunter family are the arrogant, powerful masters of Clough Grange. Their feuds are sparked by a generation of guilt, despair and ill-fortune. But their passions are awakened by the arrival of nineteen-year-old Kate Weatherby.

A VENETIAN RECKONING
Donna Leon

When the body of a prominent international lawyer is found in the carriage of an intercity train, Commissario Guido Brunetti begins to dig deeper into the secret lives of the once great and good.

A TASTE FOR DEATH
Peter O'Donnell

Modesty Blaise and Willie Garvin take on impossible odds in the shape of Simon Delicata, the man with a taste for death, and Swordmaster, Wenczel, in a terrifying duel. Finally, in the Sahara desert, the intrepid pair must summon every killing skill to survive.

SEVEN DAYS FROM MIDNIGHT
Rona Randall

In the Comet Theatre, London, seven people have good reason for wanting beautiful Maxine Culver out of the way. Each one has reason to fear her blackmail. But whose shadow is it that lurks in the wings, waiting to silence her once and for all?

QUEEN OF THE ELEPHANTS
Mark Shand

Mark Shand knows about the ways of elephants, but he is no match for the tiny Parbati Barua, the daughter of India's greatest expert on the Asian elephant, the late Prince of Gauripur, who taught her everything. Shand sought out Parbati to take part in a film about the plight of the wild herds today in north-east India.

THE DARKENING LEAF
Caroline Stickland

On storm-tossed Chesil Bank in 1847, the young lovers, Philobeth and Frederick, prevent wreckers mutilating the apparent corpse of a young woman. Discovering she is still alive, Frederick takes her to his grandmother's home. But the rescue is to have violent and far-reaching effects . . .

A WOMAN'S TOUCH
Emma Stirling

When Fenn went to stay on her uncle's farm in Africa, the lovely Helena Starr seemed to resent her — especially when Dr Jason Kemp agreed to Fenn helping in his bush hospital. Though it seemed Jason saw Fenn as little more than a child, her feelings for him were those of a woman.

A DEAD GIVEAWAY
Various Authors

This book offers the perfect opportunity to sample the skills of five of the finest writers of crime fiction — Clare Curzon, Gillian Linscott, Peter Lovesey, Dorothy Simpson and Margaret Yorke.

DOUBLE INDEMNITY — MURDER FOR INSURANCE
Jad Adams

This is a collection of true cases of murderers who insured their victims then killed them — or attempted to. Each tense, compelling account tells a story of cold-blooded plotting and elaborate deception.

THE PEARLS OF COROMANDEL
By Keron Bhattacharya

John Sugden, an ambitious young Oxford graduate, joins the Indian Civil Service in the early 1920s and goes to uphold the British Raj. But he falls in love with a young Hindu girl and finds his loyalties tragically divided.

WHITE HARVEST
Louis Charbonneau

Kathy McNeely, a marine biologist, sets out for Alaska to carry out important research. But when she stumbles upon an illegal ivory poaching operation that is threatening the world's walrus population, she soon realises that she will have to survive more than the harsh elements . . .

TO THE GARDEN ALONE
Eve Ebbett

Widow Frances Morley's short, happy marriage was childless, and in a succession of borders she attempts to build a substitute relationship for the husband and family she does not have. Over all hovers the shadow of the man who terrorized her childhood.

CONTRASTS
Rowan Edwards

Julia had her life beautifully planned — she was building a thriving pottery business as well as sharing her home with her friend Pippa, and having fun owning a goat. But the goat's problems brought the new local vet, Sebastian Trent, into their lives.

MY OLD MAN AND THE SEA
David and Daniel Hays

Some fathers and sons go fishing together. David and Daniel Hays decided to sail a tiny boat seventeen thousand miles to the bottom of the world and back. Together, they weave a story of travel, adventure, and difficult, sometimes terrifying, sailing.